Ayisha Malik's novels *Sofia Khan is Not Obliged*, *The Other Half of Happiness* and *This Green and Pleasant Land* were met with great critical acclaim.

Ayisha won Best Adult Book in the 2020 Diverse Book Awards and she has been shortlisted for the Asian Women of Achievement Award.

She lives in North London.

By Ayisha Malik

Sofia Khan novels:

Sofia Khan is Not Obliged

The Other Half of Happiness

Sofia Khan and the Baby Blues
(Quick Reads short story)

This Green and Pleasant Land

The Movement

SOFIA KHAN AND THE BABY BLUES

Ayisha Malik

REVIEW

First published in paperback in Great Britain in 2022
by HEADLINE REVIEW
an imprint of HEADLINE PUBLISHING GROUP

1

Cataloguing in Publication Data is available from the British Library

ISBN 978 1 4722 8457 0

Typeset in Stone Serif by CC Book Production

Printed and bound in Great Britain by Clays Ltd, Elcograf S.p.A.

MIX
Paper from
responsible sources
FSC® C104740

Headline's policy is to use papers that are natural,
renewable and recyclable products and made from wood grown
in well-managed forests and other controlled sources. The logging
and manufacturing processes are expected to conform to the
environmental regulations of the country of origin.

HEADLINE PUBLISHING GROUP
An Hachette UK Company
Carmelite House
50 Victoria Embankment
London EC4Y 0DZ

www.headline.co.uk
www.hachette.co.uk

To my friend, Alicia,
for being mine and Sofia's biggest fan.

JANUARY
Begin Again

Friday 1st January

Moving back in with your mum in your 40s is a bit of a ball-ache. Especially when you need earplugs so you don't hear what is going on in the bedroom between your mum and your step-dad.

I wonder what the rules are about wearing a hijab in front of step-dads? But who has time to worry about a piece of cloth on their head when their baby won't stop crying?

(Might have a minute to worry about hijab when Amelia is eighteen.)

'*Oof*,' yelled Mum, bursting into my childhood bedroom, hair a mess, bosom wobbling under her dressing gown. '*The baby*,' she added, as if I didn't know Amelia was crying blue murder in her cot.

Then my step-dad, Mehboob (or Moobs as I like to call him), appeared behind my mum (no messy hair which is a perk of being bald) and put a hand on her shoulder.

Ugh.

I might be forty, but seeing a man who is

not your father touching your mum would be *vom* for anyone. I have matured in other ways (note: baby) but perhaps not in *every* way.

Actually, before Mum came barging in, I was standing by the window looking over at Conall's house next door. Well, at the back garden, which is all I can see from my window. The house where my first ex-husband used to live, which is now (because his tenants have moved out) as empty as my soul, some might say.

Mum gave me a suspicious look. She's seen me staring at his home, and she makes subtle comments like, *'That's what happens when you marry a white person.'*

I don't know what his being white has to do with the ex-wife and son he never told me about. All those secrets that led to our divorce.

It didn't matter that he had converted to Islam. Which is still probably the most romantic thing anyone's ever done for me.

Anyway, after him I *did* marry the ideal brown man and look how that turned out . . .

Mum came over and looked at Amelia.

'Don't,' I whispered. But it was too late. Amelia had stopped crying and was now looking up at Mum in mild wonder. (Which is a look a lot of people have when they're with my mum.)

'Mehnaz,' said my dad's stand-in. 'Let's leave them.'

Horny bastard.

Then my mum looked at me with the usual dismay.

'*This* is what you left Sakeb for? A crying baby?'

My second husband, Sakeb, had different ideas about being a parent. He wanted me to have children in the usual way. Sex. Pregnancy. Labour. That kind of thing. I wanted to adopt a child who was already in a world that didn't want it. Surely that makes more sense? There are already so *many* babies. I, myself, tried to be Muslim about it (looking after orphans/children in need is something every Muslim should do. Possibly could get you a ticket to heaven. Excellent.) But raising another person's child wasn't Sakeb's idea of being spiritual.

Something he and my mum have in common.

But I couldn't change the way I thought or felt, just because my (second) husband wanted me to.

There are limits to what one should do for another.

'She is *my* crying baby,' I replied to Mum now, picking up Amelia (or Millie as I like to call her) and kissing her on her chubby cheek.

I had wanted to foster and adopt an older child, but I got a three-month-old (now nine months). Officially, I'm her permanent foster-carer. You can imagine how happy my mum and step-dad were about all the training and interviews they had to have. But when you want something, you have to fight for it.

Now, Mum just humph'ed and pushed Moobs out of the room. She gave me and my bad decisions a backward glance.

It wasn't a great living set-up, for any of us, but I didn't get any money from the divorce because we just had an Islamic marriage. Apart from the *mahar* which is money promised to a bride. It's agreed upon by both parties before the marriage. She can ask for it at any point during the marriage. Or if there's a divorce. So I got all of five hundred pounds. Should've known back then that he was a tight bastard. We were always meant to register and then never did. And I always felt too guilty (leaving him for a baby) to ask for what was rightfully mine.

It's my fault for thinking that the second marriage would last. Somewhere in my brain, I thought marrying someone I loved less than Conall would make for a happier time.

I laid Millie down next to me on the bed. Something you're obviously never meant to do, but she smells so lovely and her cheeks are so cute. When she looks at me with her brown eyes . . . well, my heart can still feel things at least.

'You are worth more than a thousand men,' I whispered to her.

Eventually, she fell asleep and I looked out of the window at Conall's house again. Now *he* would've loved Millie. He wouldn't have chosen divorce over me and a child. But then his life was so mixed-up – *he* was so mixed-up. Plus, he had *lied* to me. How was I meant to forgive him for hiding the fact that he'd had an ex-wife and a child?

A child that he had abandoned.

I know he was sorry about it. I know he felt regret about not being a proper father to his son. I know he had his issues, but still . . .

The truth is I should've waited longer to marry Conall. But nope. I just had to rush in, didn't I? Because *Oh, I love him. And oh, we're Muslim. And, oh, no sex before marriage.*

So, let's just get hitched and hope everything else falls into place.

Ugh! Beliefs can make a person stupid.

But then I married Sakeb. Someone I *did* know and that hardly worked out. So really, whichever way you do it, you're buggered.

I laid back down next to Millie.

The trouble with decisions is you never know which one is going to turn out to be a mistake.

Sunday 10th January

Mum and Moobs were having some kind of argument when I walked into the house with Millie in the stroller. Every time I used to see Moobs I'd feel annoyed. It happened more when I'd come over (when I was still married to Sakeb) and I'd notice there were fewer and fewer pictures of my actual dad. How could you remove over thirty years' worth of marriage? It's been ten years since he died, but I can't believe how few signs of him are left in the home. Just some photos of him with us as children. And one at my sister Maria's wedding.

God, I missed her. She is now living her family life in Dubai.

The thing no one tells you about being twice-divorced and having a foster-soon-to-be-adopted baby is that everyone else is going through their own version of a family drama.

Because of this, no one has time for yours. The friends that used to be on hotline don't respond to messages at once any more. No more same-day delivery of feelings. No one tells you how quickly it all changes. How much *you* will change.

Your 20s and 30s are basically just constant self-obsession.

'Auntie and Uncle Bhatt are coming for dinner,' said Mum, watching me trying to get Millie out of her coat.

Moobs walked past me with a grumpy face.

'Mum,' I said. 'Not again. All they're going to do is ask how I'm going to plan my future now I've left my *second* husband. And really, I get enough of that from you.'

'They ask the right question!' she said.

She was frying onions. Another side-effect of being home is that Millie and I smell like we live in an Indian takeaway. Moobs left to get drinks for tonight. The Rubicon juice kind, of course.

'Make sure it's *light*,' said Mum as he left. 'You've seen how big his belly is getting?'

It took some effort not to look at Mum's own belly.

I made up a bottle for Millie. Mum huffed as she looked between me, Millie resting on my hip, and the box of Cow & Gate.

'You know their cousin's son is just divorced too,' said Mum. 'He has two children, but you can't be fussy any more.'

'Mum . . .'

'Has Sakeb been in touch?' she asked.

'Why would he?' I replied. 'I've left the business. I'm starting out on my own.'

Which is what I told myself, but the only thing I was doing was reading up on when babies start to walk and talk. Sakeb was in the process of buying me out of the publishing house we'd set up. Nine months later and he is still no closer to giving me what is mine, which is why I am living in my childhood bedroom with a baby.

If I wanted, I could actually break down and cry right now. But I have Millie on my hip, so that'll have to wait for later.

*

Oh my good God. I'd put Millie down for her nap and could hear Uncle Bhatt and Moobs with their loud laughter. I marched downstairs, hands on hips like a prison guard and said: '*The baby's sleeping.*'

Having a baby can turn you into a real bore.

Everyone cleared their throats. Mum looked annoyed (but that's nothing new since I've moved in), Moobs looked bored (also more often since I've moved in).

I went back upstairs and sat in my mum's room because I didn't want to disturb Millie in mine. I really need to get my own place, but *how, how, how* do I do that with no money? I can't find a proper job, because finding one is a full-time job in itself.

Millie takes up all my time and childcare is so expensive. And Mum won't look after her because she's *'the reason I have another failed marriage'*. I don't even want to ask for her help. I was ill one week and that was the only time Mum took Millie out to the park, fed her, changed her nappy. It made me cry for a good ten minutes.

All the time I try not to think about Conall. But it's so much harder when, every time I leave the house, I'm reminded of all the times he and I would stand outside our homes and talk. I'd tell him what my family's latest madness was, and he'd laugh. All those times I went to his house as I wrote my book.

And I miss my friends. It takes weeks to actually plan a date to get together, and then one cancels so everyone has to cancel . . .

Ooh, *Fozia's actually calling.*

'Darling,' she said warmly.

I could hear Zara, my unofficial god-child, in the background shouting, 'Mummy! Mummy!'

'Mummy's on the phone, darling,' she said to her whining four-year-old.

'Look at my drawiwing.'

'Isn't that beautiful,' replied Foz. 'You're a *very* clever girl, aren't you?'

'Who are you speaking to?' Zara whined.

God, kids are annoying.

'Auntie Sofia. We miss her, don't we?'

'No,' my god-child replied.

'Right, now let Mummy speak to Auntie Sofia. We haven't spoken in a very long time and let's face it, her life is a bit of a mess right now.'

'I can be her friend,' said Zara.

'Please, make my life worse,' I said into the phone.

Foz laughed. 'Bloody kids,' she whispered as Zara had waddled away. 'Bugger off and let me talk. I'm telling you, one is fine, two is mad, but three . . . ? What the hell was I thinking?'

'No one who has babies is thinking,' I said.

'How are you anyway?'

'Amelia's asleep and the Bhatts are over for dinner, so I'm naturally hiding in my mum's room.'

'Oh.'

'It's like it's 2010 . . . only I have wrinkles and a baby,' I said.

'Hmm.'

'I really want a fag but I can't smoke in the same house as the baby.'

'The things we have to give up,' replied Foz. She paused.

'I'm worried about you,' she said eventually.

My eyes filled with tears, which is stupid because I'm fine really. I'm *fine*.

'Don't be. I'm *fine*.'

'Shut the hell up.'

I let out a laugh.

Just then, I heard shouting from the street. I looked out onto the lamp-lit road at the people making the noise.

'*What the hell?*' I said from behind the curtain.

A huge removal van had parked in the middle of the road and some guy behind was stuck and shouting at the driver.

Who was moving next door? Whoever it was, if they woke my baby up they were about to get an earful.

'I have to go,' I said to Foz, who couldn't hear the drama over her own kids who were now in a full-blown row with one another (Zara had just hit her younger sister with a truck).

13

I stormed down the stairs, ignoring the guests and Mum calling out for me to stay indoors, and went outside.

'Excuse me!' I said to the mad driver behind the truck. 'I have a baby sleeping indoors. Lower your voice.'

He then shouted about the removal man parking in the middle of the road.

'Just *reverse*,' I said.

People were real idiots.

'You reverse yourself inside,' he said.

The nerve.

I strode closer towards him. 'Are you *actually* stupid?'

He came up to me and I realised Mum, Moobs and the Bhatts were now standing at the front door.

'Listen, *lady*, this is none of your business. This ma—'

'Step back from my daughter.'

Mum had come up next to me and was now pointing her finger at the man.

'Who the f—'

Just then a tall figure loomed over my mum and me.

'Listen here, you get back in your car, reverse like a man with some sense, and step away from these ladies.'

14

My heart stopped. Actually stopped. For a moment, I couldn't even look up. I would know that voice anywhere. Mum, however, didn't miss a beat.

'*Colin*,' she exclaimed.

I dared to look his way.

There he was, all six feet and bulk of him (bulkier than when I had last seen him seven years ago).

My mouth was dry, my breath caught in my throat.

'Conall, Mum,' I said. '*Conall*.'

The angry man looked up at Conall and hesitated. It was about three degrees outside but Conall was in jeans and a t-shirt, his tattoos going all up around his arms.

'Step away,' Conall added, moving forward.

The man muttered something under his breath before he turned around. He got back into his car and reversed at manic speed until he was out of sight.

I realised I was shivering.

'You'd better get inside,' said Conall. 'You'll catch a cold.'

Mum's eyes narrowed at him. 'He's right.'

She grabbed my arm and began to drag me indoors. Towards Moobs and the Bhatts. I felt like I was in a Bollywood film, being pulled away from the love of my life. (In a dramatic sense, I had loved Conall. A lot. But he hadn't been *the love of my life*. Obviously. The man you divorce can't be. There never would be a love of my life, and that's fine because some things are more important.)

'*I'm not cold*,' I called out, as Mum managed to get me through the front gate. '*You're* cold.'

Unfortunately, it's all I could think of saying.

And there it was. The bloody thing that made my stomach flip every time I saw it – his hard, unreadable face, turning into a smile, a glint in his eye.

The problem is, when you've shared intimate things with a man, every look ends up having a double meaning.

God, I still fancied him.

ARGH.

I managed to get out of Mum's grip and stopped at the gate. This *must* be a dream.

Then Mum grabbed my arm again.

Before I turned around to go back into the house, a figure walked up to him. At first I thought it was the removal man, but the walk was too much like a young person's. It was a boy.

'Dad. The guy's asking where to put the coffee table.'

It was his son. Eamonn.

What was he doing with Conall?

What was Conall doing here?

Then I heard a wail come from inside the house.

Everyone looked towards it. Including Conall.

His expression changed to something else.

Wonder?

Disappointment?

Millie had woken up. To a bit of a nightmare.

FEBRUARY
Fate Doesn't Count

Wednesday 3rd February

Cannot believe my first ex-husband is living next door to me. *Again.*

I suppose history does repeat itself.

Between crying baby and my own confusion, I had to dictate a message to Foz (hands being full of Millie) to tell her what the hell had happened.

She called me straight away. I had to decline it because Millie was nodding off.

'Oh my God, it's *fate*!' she shrieked on a voice message.

I deleted it. I don't need that kind of thinking saved on my phone.

It's been over three weeks and I still haven't gone over to speak to Conall. It's not like he's come around here. I mean, you'd think after the lies he'd told me, he'd pop in to say sorry about ruining my life.

Ha! Fate! As if.

Friday 5th February

Argh! *Fate*. Bloody parcel came for me and there was no one home, so the postman left it with *the next-door neighbour*. There should be a rule against this type of thing.

I paced the room, carrying Millie, obsessing over whether I should go or send Mum. Of course, it was clear which was the lesser of two evils.

'Your mum needs to get over it, doesn't she?' I said to Millie. 'Women in their 40s should behave like women in their 40s and not get caught up in silly dramas.'

I sighed. I now had the future generation to think about. I mean, if I behaved like a self-obsessed idiot, then what hope would there be for Millie?

So, I took Millie (and a deep breath) and knocked on Conall's door.

Eamonn opened it. His dark hair tied back in a bun. A little patch of wiry hair on his chin. He was, what? Fifteen, sixteen now? He was about four inches shorter than Conall and, unlike Conall, was very thin. His pale skin flushed red.

Was he embarrassed? Annoyed? Who could tell?

I smiled. Maybe too widely. He looked at me, confused. Maybe it was my hijab?

Or maybe it was just me.

'Hello,' I said, unable to stop showing my teeth.

Nothing.

Millie reached her hand out to him and gurgled. He stared at her like she was an alien. (To be fair, kids can be alien-like.)

I took a deep breath (again) and asked: 'Is . . .'

Conall?

Your dad?

All these decisions!

'Your dad home? I think a parcel was left for me?'

Eamonn closed the door and I wasn't sure whether he'd ever open it again. A few minutes later he came back and gave me the parcel. Millie snatched it, grabbing the corner and putting it in her mouth. I thought Eamonn almost smiled.

Almost.

We all know that doesn't count.

I looked over his shoulder for signs of Conall. Nothing.

I should've been glad.

I *was* glad.

Yet I couldn't move.

'How are you?' I asked carefully.

'Fine,' he grunted.

'Settling in okay?'

He just stared at me. And as I looked over his shoulder again, he slammed the door in mine and Millie's faces.

I looked at Millie. 'Well, guess I have this to look forward to with you.'

She grabbed my face and drooled on her bib. It's the only thing that made me laugh that morning.

*

I don't thank God often enough for Mum's husband, but I thanked Him today when they'd both gone to someone's for dinner. Millie and I were home alone. I put her to bed and went into the living room to read an actual book. But I couldn't focus, so I watched television. (*What is television any more?*)

At one point I closed my eyes, just to take in the peace and quiet. And then in the middle of the quiet, out of nowhere, I felt lonely. As if I was the only person in the world. A silly thing to feel when my baby was upstairs. But how can feelings be helped?

I *was* alone.

I'd have gone out and had a cigarette if I still smoked.

The things you do for love.

Then the doorbell rang.

I sprang up, worried it would wake Millie.

'Oh,' I said, as I opened the door.

It was Conall.

I felt something catch in my throat.

'Hi.'

'Hello,' he replied.

We both stood there for a while, quiet.

'You got your parcel?' he asked.

'Yes. Eamonn was very helpful.'

Conall raised his eyebrows.

'Doesn't talk much, does he?' I said. 'Guess he takes after his dad.'

'Are you alone?' Conall asked.

Yes, I am all alone!

I realised I didn't have my hijab on, but I figure Conall's seen more than my head of hair so who cares. I opened the door.

He came in and looked around the house he'd been welcomed into all those years ago.

'It's changed,' he said, walking into the living room.

'Yep.'

He sat down, making himself comfortable, but I was still standing, arms crossed.

'So, you have yourself a baby?' he said.

I nodded.

He cleared his throat. Paused. Cleared it again.

'And where's . . . what's his name?' he asked.

'Sakeb?'

'That's the one.'

'I don't know,' I replied.

There was a long pause.

'Sit down, Sofe.'

I wasn't sure, but thought that staying standing just because he told me to take a seat was probably childish.

'Do you want tea?' I asked.

'Not the way you make it,' he said with a grin.

I, despite myself, laughed. 'Make it your bloody self then.'

And he did. He came back a few minutes later with two cups.

We sat in silence for a while before he spoke. 'I'm sorry I didn't come and see you sooner.'

'Is that all you're sorry for?' I replied.

He shook his head. 'You know that's not true.'

And the thing I suddenly realised then, is that perhaps motherhood has taken away my ability to hold a grudge. Or be angry.

'I know,' I said eventually. 'Still, it would be good to hear it.'

He put his tea down, took my cup and put it down too, and grabbed my hands. He looked at me for so long I thought he was going to bloody kiss me!

'I have never been sorrier for anything in my life,' he said, eventually.

It took a fair bit for me not to burst into tears. I had imagined this moment in my head many times, and not in a single one was I unable to speak, let me tell you. Why was I even thinking about him kissing me? (I should add that I had also imagined *that* many times, and each time I would turn away. I would say, *it's too late*, and then walk away. Of course, in reality, I was glued to the sofa and choking on my own words.)

'Sofe?'

'Mmm.'

He paused. 'Just that . . . in so many ways it's worked out the way it was meant to.'

'Hmm?'

'I'll always be sorry I wasn't honest with you, but I've got a second chance with Eamonn now.'

And just like that he let go of my hands (and the hope that he would kiss me. Oh dear, oh dear).

Then he leaned back and told me what had happened. Eamonn's mum, who had been a single mother for so many years, had met someone. Eamonn wasn't happy at home any more. He was getting more and more difficult. Staying out late, bad company. His mother couldn't take it and so Conall swept in. He said that he would take Eamonn to London and be the father that he hadn't been when his son was growing up.

'She said no at first, obviously,' he said. 'Whatever else you might say about her, she loves Eamonn something fierce.' He paused. 'But that kid – he was just going off the rails and I had to do something. I've taken time off work. I'm doing enough to pay the bills, but now I can spend more time with him.'

I nodded. 'And how's it going?'

'Have no idea. He hardly speaks to me.'

I felt such a pain for Conall in that moment. To have a child that *should* be mad at you. Eamonn has every right. Conall messed up. Still . . . I couldn't help but feel for him. People make mistakes. It's how we try to fix them that should matter.

That's the idea, at least.

'It'll be okay,' I said. 'You always were good at talking people around.'

'Like you?'

I laughed. 'I didn't take much convincing though, in the end.'

He looked at me for a moment, and I'm not sure what it meant. And I didn't have a chance to find out as Millie started crying.

I settled her down and came back into the living room. Conall was twisting his cup of tea in his hand. A habit he always had.

'When does Sakeb have her?' he asked.

For a moment I was confused. But of course, why would he know Millie wasn't biologically mine?

'Oh, no,' I said. 'He doesn't have her.'

Now Conall looked confused.

'I mean, she's not *his*,' I continued, which just seemed to confuse him further. 'What I mean is, I'm adopting her.'

Quiet.

'Paperwork takes ages but I'm her permanent foster-carer. You can imagine my mum's thrilled.'

Why wasn't he speaking?

'And well, Sakeb was *so* pleased that he asked for a divorce so ... here I am,' I added, gesturing to my mum's house.

It took a few minutes before he spoke. 'You got divorced because you wanted to adopt?'

'Some people call me crazy.'

'Well, *he* was. For letting you go.'

Oh dear. Feelings.

Why are there feelings?

'I think it was more to do with the fact that I make shit tea, to be honest,' I said dryly.

Conall let out a small laugh. 'Valid reason, if you ask me.'

We sat in silence for a while before he spoke again. 'You're happy now?'

What could I say to that? Didn't he see my situation? Who *would* be happy? But then, what did that have to do with anything? Your own happiness hardly matters when you have a baby. Everything is about them. You put your sadness to one side and you *focus*. Focus is key.

'I have the best thing in the world now,' I said. 'What could I be unhappy about?'

'You didn't answer the question.'

'Are *you*?' I asked.

He paused. 'Right now I am.'

I thought my heart might pop out of my chest.

'Not everyone gets second chances,' he said.

I swallowed hard. Could this be it? Could this be our second chance?

'And this time,' he added. 'I'm not messing

up with Eamonn. He's coming first. With everything.'

I gripped my cup. *Of course.* Eamonn. One can be as self-obsessed in their 40s as they were in their 20s.

'And he should,' I said. 'For better or for worse, the kids always end up coming first.'

Conall looked at me again. In that way he always has, as if trying to read my mind and honestly, more often than not, I feel like he *can*. I had to look away.

'Yeah. They do,' he said.

He went to leave but stopped at the door. 'You're doing an amazing thing here, Sofe.'

'Am I?'

'You know you are.'

I shook my head. 'When you do the things you want to do, they don't feel amazing. Just necessary.' I paused. 'Millie is necessary.'

He leaned in and kissed me on my cheek. I breathed in his soapy scent and he stayed there, just a little longer than perhaps he needed to, before he closed the door behind him.

Perhaps he felt that was necessary for me too.

*

I messaged Foz to tell her what happened, but she hasn't replied yet.

31

For a moment I thought about not washing my face. Letting the smell of him linger.

But just because love is idiotic, it doesn't mean I have to be.

Saturday 20th February

I have been blindsided! Bloody, bloody guests. New ones come almost *every* weekend and honestly, it's all I can do not to chuck samosas at them. To make it worse, while I was getting ready (because apparently pyjamas is not acceptable clothing) Mum had taken Millie and given her to Conall to babysit for the evening.

'Mum!' I protested, 'I'll have to put her to bed and why on earth would you give my baby to my ex-husband just because we have guests?'

Mum seemed to hesitate. Unusual for her.

Moobs walked past the bedroom, singing an old Bollywood song. Mum looked at him fondly.

'I told Conall . . .' began Mum.

'You told Conall . . . ?'

'That there is a *rishta* coming for you today.

Conall ruined your life so he can at least look after your baby for a few hours.'

Rishta?

A potential man to marry??

What in the name of all that is holy???

'Mum!'

I feel like I shout at Mum (and generally) a lot nowadays. Surprised I haven't lost my voice.

'Are you actually mad?' I said through gritted teeth. 'You're setting me up with someone without telling me, and pretending that I don't have a baby? How dumb is this man that if we got married he wouldn't notice *a child*.'

Mum paused. Moobs' singing (now coming from downstairs) got louder.

'You haven't adopted her *yet*,' Mum replied, finally.

I stared at her. It was more than one could take. Sakeb never accepted Millie and nor would my mother. All it did was make me love Millie even more. I turned away from Mum and marched down the stairs, ready to bring Millie back from Conall's at once when the bloody guests rang the doorbell. Moobs gave me such a deathly stare that I almost wondered if he'd throw a samosa at *me*.

God, I missed my dad.

'For once, think of your mother,' he said,

voice lowered. 'Has she ever stopped you from doing what you want?'

'I'm *forty*,' I said.

'You are *Pakistani*. And still her daughter. And in *our* house.'

'*Her* house,' I corrected.

The doorbell rang again. I heard Mum exclaim '*Oof.*'

Moobs stepped back. 'I can't force you to do anything. But your mother has been very upset. It is hard for other people too.'

So much to think about!

I can't believe Conall agreed to look after Millie, and I don't know why it gave me a sense of comfort, knowing that Millie was spending time with him. I wouldn't trust anyone else.

'Millie will officially be my baby soon,' I said.

He nodded.

'So you *have* to talk Mum round,' I added.

He paused. 'Yes. Yes, I will. I am already trying.'

For a moment, I almost felt some affection for him. Even though he was blackmailing me into staying quiet this evening.

'Okay,' I replied.

Then I opened the door to potential husband number three.

*

We can safely say that potential husband number three will *not* be potential divorcee number three. I dropped in, early on in the conversation, that I had a baby that I was trying to adopt.

There was silence. When the guests left, I strode over to Conall's to bring my baby back. My mum was talking non-stop about me ruining my chances of marital bliss, while Moobs cleared the table of tea and samosas.

'I cannot believe her,' I said, as soon as I walked into Conall's.

It was almost like it was ten years ago.

'No marriage number three then?' he asked.

'You think it's funny?'

He laughed and shook his head. 'No, no. I took it very seriously when your mam said the very least I could do is babysit your child while you get set up with another man.'

'Conall.'

'I could imagine your reaction.'

'It was ridiculous,' I said.

'Her heart's in the right place.'

'Trust me, it's not her heart. She just wants me out of the house so she can live in wedded bliss with her own husband.' I paused, watching the look on his face. 'Yes, I know. She has a right to be happy too.'

I walked through the hallway, asking how Millie had been. When I turned into the living room, I found Eamonn playing peek-a-boo with her. I looked at Conall, who raised his eyebrows. Eamonn hadn't noticed us, so I pushed Conall towards the kitchen.

'What's going on in there?'

'Honestly,' said Conall. 'Like a duck to water. He's been hanging out with her all evening. She seems to love it.'

I poked my head into the room again and back out. 'He's *smiling*.'

Unfortunately, the smile disappeared as soon as Eamonn saw me.

'Thanks for entertaining her,' I said, picking Millie up.

She reached an arm out to Eamonn, but he was already strolling out of the room, back hunched.

'Bye,' I called out to him, but he ignored me.

'Sorry,' said Conall. He looked embarrassed.

'Oh, don't worry.' I hesitated. 'But it's not like you to let someone get away with that sort of behaviour.'

Conall stuck his hands in his pockets.

'Anyway,' I said. 'Thanks again for looking after her. I'm now going to go home and tell my mother off. Again.'

'Sofe,' said Conall, as I was about to leave.
'Yeah?'
He paused. 'Bring her over more often.'
For a minute, I thought how nice that would
be. I had this picture of me and Conall sat
drinking tea while Eamonn played peek-a-boo
with Millie. Then I realised that you can't
pretend to be a family with someone. No matter
how much you like the idea.

*

I returned home to Mum who was still in a
strop. Just as I was about to go to bed, she
helpfully said, 'You are ruining your life, I hope
you know that. And next month you will have
to behave yourself.'
'Why?'
'Mehboob's nephew is coming to stay.'
Oh good God, *more* guests.
'He's a doctor,' she added.
As if that somehow made up for it.
I need to get out of this place.

MARCH

Lessons in Laughter

Saturday 13th March

Someone please save me. I have Millie crying her eyes out every time she sees Moobs' nephew, Adam (trust baby's instincts), Mum hurrying around cooking food and only taking a breath to tell me off for something or other, while Moobs and Adam sit nice and cosy, in the living room, laughing and chatting.

I wouldn't care, only Adam keeps knocking on my bedroom door every five minutes asking questions.

Where are the towels?

Can you turn the heating up?

Where's the closest train station?

What are good sights to see in London?

Should the baby be crying like that?

She wouldn't be bloody crying if you didn't keep showing your face in the room! And ever heard of Google??

Mum came in and told me to try and be more helpful. She ignored Millie being red in the face with tears.

'Since the baby you have become very *sarri*,' Mum said, raising her voice.

Which loosely translates to a raging sourpuss.

Perhaps she had a point. I don't think I smile or laugh as often. Which is ironic, given I have the lines to prove that I must have been quite good at laughing.

'What do you *want*, baby?' I said to Millie, who was now so red in the face I thought she might stop breathing.

She wasn't taking her milk. I'd fed her and changed her nappy. I had taken her for a walk when she had just burst into tears and she hasn't stopped since. I got a sinking feeling in my stomach. What if she died? Of course, I have this fear every night when I put her to bed. Sometimes I randomly wake up, just to check she's still breathing.

'Oof,' added Mum. 'How loud.'

'Yes, *thanks*, Mum, that's really helpful,' I said, my voice almost breaking.

Mum hesitated for a moment, before she took Millie from me and checked her face, smelled her nappy.

'What's wrong, hmm?' Mum was frowning as she spoke, but her voice, shockingly, was soft.

Millie continued to cry.

'I don't understand,' I said, almost breaking

into a sob myself. 'She was fine and then we're almost home and she just started.'

'Oh, ho-ho-ho,' said Mum, like Santa, resting Millie against her.

She swayed her from side to side, trying to shush her.

That's when I did cry. Why couldn't Mum be like this all the time?

'O-ho,' said Mum. 'If you cry, she will cry more. Control yourself, Sofia.'

Mum turned Millie away from me, when sodding Adam knocked on the door again.

'Can I help?' he asked.

He was such a tiny, little man I wondered why Millie didn't like him.

I almost shut the door in his face before she looked at him and cried harder, but he'd already come in and taken her from Mum.

'Shh, shh, shh,' he said, wiping her brow.

'He's a doctor,' Mum whispered.

She'd mentioned that a few hundred times. He took off Millie's tights and inspected her legs, then her bare arms, until he found a huge red welt.

'Looks like she's been bitten.'

Oh my actual God.

'Don't worry,' he said. 'I'll run out and get medicine. Just keep holding her until I'm back.'

I did as I was told. Mum even brought me some Guava Rubicon.

'It's light,' she added.

Adam was back within ten minutes, applying lotion to the bite. It took around twenty minutes, but Millie finally calmed down. I kissed her head and rocked her back and forth until she finally fell asleep.

'Thank you so much,' I whispered to Adam, as we left the room.

'No problem. Maybe now you'll tell me the best way to get to Big Ben.'

I laughed.

'You can go somewhere a little more interesting than that,' I said.

And then a miracle! Mum *volunteered* to babysit so I could take Adam out. It had been such a day, and the sun was out for the first time in months. I felt relieved.

When was the last time I'd had the chance to see my beloved city? I even wore *make-up*.

Maybe Adam isn't so bad after all.

*

Adult company! Excellent evening. Adam quite funny. Came home around midnight. Looked up at Conall's and saw the curtain twitch. Hope I wasn't laughing too loudly.

Thursday 18th March

Oh my actual God. Woke up and saw Millie's cot was empty. Had wild panic that someone had crawled through my bedroom window and kidnapped her. Hurried down the stairs, hair a mess, unwashed face, only to see Adam feeding her a bottle! I looked at the time. It was nine o'clock in the morning.

'Why did no one wake me up?' I exclaimed.

Mum walked into the living room and handed Adam a cup of tea.

'Your mum said you always wake up early. So I suggested she bring Millie downstairs so you could have a lie-in.'

Mum looked me up and down. Then she nodded at a) my coming downstairs scarfless and b) looking like a complete mess.

'You don't mind, do you?' asked Adam.

I guess Millie wasn't crying now because she had a bottle shoved in her face. So, to avoid my mum's death stares, I changed and came back downstairs. Millie was now in her bouncy chair watching the 'Baby Shark' song on TV.

Oh dear.

Mum was in the kitchen while Moobs had gone to the shops.

'Thanks for that,' I said to Adam.

He raised his hands as if it was nothing. 'I was telling Auntie what a great thing you're doing.'

I wish everyone would stop saying that.

'And she agreed,' he added.

I whipped my head around from watching five grown adults on TV dancing around in tutus.

'Don't be so surprised,' he said. 'I told her there aren't many women who would do what you did. Especially considering . . .'

'The second divorce?'

He looked at the ground and then back up at me. I wondered if he'd watched a lot of Bollywood films. He seemed to be playing a part. Then I told the voice in my head to shut up. Sometimes people are nice just because that's who they are.

'Thanks,' I said. 'Even though it means I have no money now and am living with Mum and your uncle.'

It hit me how I've been complaining about the same bloody thing for months now. I used to be a woman who *did* things. Being home's almost made me forget who I am. Or used to be.

And that's when I decided to get off my arse and do something about my situation.

Well, only because Adam offered to look after Millie while I did so.

Friday 19th March

Took my laptop, left the house and went to the coffee shop around the corner. Started working on a website yesterday to bring in more freelance work to make some bloody money, so I can move out of my mother's home. I'd been there for a few hours when Conall walked in.

He looked around in mild panic. 'Where's the baby?'

'I left her in the Post Office,' I replied. 'Don't worry, they said they'd order a tracked delivery.'

'Coffee perked you up then?' he said with a smile. 'What are you doing here?'

'Trying to get my life back together. Hence the chocolate almond croissant and flat white. Which I can actually enjoy now Millie's with Adam.'

Conall's face seemed to change.

'Oh.' He hesitated. 'Well, I'll leave you to it.'

But he didn't move.

'Join me,' I said.

'Are you sure?'

Ugh. I hate my insides. They always flip at the worst time. And his bloody face. It's so kind and friendly when he smiles like that. It makes me forget how angry I was with him. And that I can't ever forgive him. Obviously. But we can still be friends. Surely.

'What are you going to do when – *whatshisname* . . . Atif?'

'Adam.'

'When he leaves?' asked Conall. 'Assuming he does. He's been there a while.'

'Are you keeping track?' I said.

Conall sipped his coffee.

'I don't know when he's leaving,' I added.

'Well, you know I'd be happy to help out with Millie. If you want. Eamonn loves her.'

'Thanks, but . . . well, last time you helped me out we know what happened.'

I fell in love with you and bloody married you.

'It wasn't that bad, was it?' he said, a smile playing on his lips.

'If it wasn't, it would've made getting over it easier.'

Sugar, caffeine and age has loosened my tongue.

Conall lowered his voice. 'I always thought you got over it pretty quick.'

Why did he sound so surprised? What did he think? People just fall in love all over the shop . . . that they don't *feel*?

'Don't fish,' I said.

'Sofe . . .'

Of course, Conall's not the fishing type. He's also not the type to offer help without meaning it.

'Would you really help with Millie?' I asked.

'Of course.'

I told him I was setting up a website for freelance work. That I needed to get my shit together so I could finally move out of Mum's. (One of us should have a happy marriage.) So I could finally hurry the adoption papers along. Eventually, Conall left me to it. A few hours later, I contacted old friends to put the word out that I, Sofia Khan, am back in business.

Monday 22ⁿᵈ March

Am beginning to think that men aren't entirely useless. Conall looked after Millie today as

Adam was out and about. Went to collect her and Eamonn was home from school. Watched her lying on her mat, playing with him as Conall took a photo. Then Millie blew a raspberry and Eamonn actually laughed out loud. He blew a raspberry back and she repeated it. Conall looked as if a miracle had taken place. We were all laughing at the raspberry exchange until I had to leave. Don't know why it made me feel sad. I wanted to sit there and watch them both for ever.

Sodding feelings.

Got several emails from potential clients. Will channel sadness into work. Like everyone else on the planet.

APRIL
Third Time Lucky

Thursday 1st April

'Is this an April Fool's, Mum?'

I was staring up at her, Millie in my arms, as I laughed out loud.

'Does my face look like it's joking?' she said.

'Not lately, Mum.'

'What is wrong with him?' she continued.

Cannot believe my mother. She is actually telling me to *marry* Adam. I mean . . . is marriage her answer to everything?

'There doesn't have to be anything wrong with him,' I said. 'I'm not ready to get married again. I'm trying to raise my baby.'

'If you adopt her, your chances of marriage will be over. You can still grab Adam while he's here.'

'*Grab* him? Mum, you've lost your mind!'

Just then Moobs walked in. 'Mehnaz, I've lost my other sock.'

One green sock with a sheep on it was hanging in his hand.

'Mehboob, forget your sock. Tell Sofia she should marry Adam.'

Millie began crying. She had the right idea.

'Mehnaz . . .' started Moobs.

Mum turned to him and his sock. 'She might not even adopt Millie if she does.'

'*Mum*. I left my last husband for her, what makes you think I'd give her up for a third one?'

'You didn't understand what you would be missing,' she said. 'Tell her, Mehboob.'

Moobs lowered the hand with the sock. 'No.'

Mum looked at him. 'What do you mean, *no*?'

It's not a word my mum's used to hearing.

'Of course Adam won't marry her,' said Moobs.

For the first time in a long time I quite liked him.

'Why *not*?' exclaimed Mum.

He lowered his voice as if that would stop me from hearing.

'Mehnaz, she's divorced. Twice. Once with a *gora*.'

Marrying a white man will often count against you.

'Are you saying she's not good enough for Adam? Have you seen how small his hands are?'

'Mum,' I said, rocking Millie. 'Just let it go. Uncle, it's fine. Mum's just being Mum.'

I went to walk away but now Mum was

full-on facing my step-dad, hands on her hips, demanding answers.

'Well?'

Just then Adam came in and asked what was going on.

'I think we should go out,' I said, putting Millie in her stroller and pulling him by the arm.

I managed to drag him through the front door, both of us leaving the drama behind.

Friday 9th April

Awkward week in the house. Mum's not talking to Moobs, and Adam doesn't understand what's happening. I keep telling Mum that he's not interested in me anyway, but she refuses to believe me. Anyway, I have applied for a part-time job with a publisher, and maybe I'll be able to leave this house and Mum's marriage obsession behind.

Sunday 25th April

Came home today to what looked like a family meeting. Mum called me inside.

'What is going on, Mehnaz?' asked Moobs, looking nervous.

His head was extra shiny. Adam was sitting, fidgeting with his hands.

'Adam,' said Mum. 'You like Sofia, yes?'

'*Mum,*' I began.

She put her hand up, as if to quieten me.

'Well, yes, Auntie,' he said. 'Of course.'

Oh, God.

'I've seen the way you look at her,' she went on.

'Who?' he asked.

'Tell your uncle you want to marry Sofia.'

I wanted to die. Actually *die.*

Adam put his small hands to his forehead.

'Auntie . . .'

'Yes . . .' said Mum, looking like she was about to win the lottery.

'I don't want to *marry* Sofia.'

I mean, it's not as if I wanted him to, but it's still a bit of a blow. Just think about his hands!

Moobs looked half-relieved and half-terrified.

'What do you *mean*?' Mum protested. 'Don't you know you can get a passport by marrying her?'

Ah. I did wonder what Mum thought Adam could possibly have to gain, but, of course, a little blue book would do it.

Who says I have no personal qualities?

Mum's shock lasted a while. Adam thought it would be a good idea to go and spend the night at a friend's house. Which, unfortunately, didn't put an end to Mum speaking (shouting) about it.

'Why didn't you say something to him?' she said to Moobs angrily. 'You were meant to be different. You are meant to *support* me.'

On and on it went. About how Moobs had disappointed her. That her first husband never supported her (emotionally) and now he turned out to be just the same.

Oh dear.

And then Moobs spoke. So quietly that Mum had to lean in and shout: '*What?*'

'But Adam is right,' replied Moobs.

He looked so sorry, even I felt bad.

'This is not a good match,' he added.

That's when the shit really hit the fan. So I took Millie and went to the only place I could to find peace away from war. Conall's.

Monday 26th April

I had told Conall why I needed refuge and he looked worried at first, and then relieved too. I mean, I know I'm no catch, but *still*. I snuck back into Mum's house, Millie asleep in my arms. It was two o'clock in the morning. Surprised Mum didn't come banging on Conall's door as she usually does.

*

Woke up the following morning to silence. That has happened zero times since I've lived in this house. Even before Millie. If there is no one speaking in loud tones, there is clattering in the kitchen, the doorbell ringing, the phone buzzing. Millie was still asleep, so I came downstairs to see that the blinds were still drawn. Mum was sitting in the semi-dark, just staring at the ground.

'Mum?' I said.

She looked up at me.

'What's happened?' I asked.

Which is when she told me that her argument with Moobs had got worse. What kind of a husband doesn't support his wife trying to get her daughter married?

'So, then what happened?' I asked, heart beating faster.

'I told him, I had a whole life of always letting things go—'

Ha!

'And I expected more from my second husband,' she added.

It wasn't the best thing to hear. My dad was obviously a brilliant father – but everyone knew he and my mum were a mismatch from hell.

She paused. 'So, I told him. If he doesn't support me then I do not need him.'

I waited for more. But she was silent.

'And . . . ?' I asked, sure that Millie would burst out crying any minute now.

'And he left.'

Oh my actual God.

Then, right on cue, Millie started crying.

MAY

All the Single Ladies

Thursday 6th May

I've never seen heartbreak in a woman in her 70s. When Dad died, Mum would cry every so often. It would be when someone spoke about him, or when she'd be telling them a story about one of their fights, or how sometimes they'd sit in the garden and sing old Bollywood songs. She'd get teary, wipe her eyes, then get up to clean the kitchen, cook food, hurry everyone into doing whatever job she had set them (I was always given the bathroom).

But in the past week and a half she's not once told me to do *anything*. She's not looked at me in disapproval, told me off for not cleaning my room, mentioned all the mistakes I've made (and we know I've made my fair share). I've even been cooking and she's not once complained about how shit it is . . .

'Shall we go for a walk, Mum?' I asked this morning.

She hasn't been to the shops in a week.

She just shook her head. I sat next to her.

'Just call him,' I said. 'He'd come back in a minute. It's just a minor argument.'

Mum shot a look at me. '*Minor?* You getting married again isn't *minor*, Sofoo.'

'Your obsession with my marriage shouldn't mean yours breaking down,' I said, which I think was quite wise and clever, to be honest.

'You wait until Amelia is older. You worry about her now?'

I nodded.

I'm scared every single day of accidentally dropping her. When she's taking the bottle, I'm worried she'll swallow the milk the wrong way. When I take her out, I have to look both ways several times in case there's a car coming. A ten-minute walk takes half an hour. Then what if she gets really ill? If she swallows something while I'm not watching and it gets stuck in her throat? What if someone kidnaps her?

All of this is made worse by the fact that the adoption papers haven't come through. What if she's taken away from me, and I don't get to worry about her for the rest of her life?

'Then you wait,' continued Mum. 'It never goes away.' She put her hand on her chest. 'You will spend the rest of your life living with your heart outside of your body.'

'I'm an adult, Mum.' I tried to reason. 'I'll be fine without a husband.'

'You can be a hundred, and I will still worry. Except, I'll be worrying from the grave. So when I marry a man that doesn't live with his heart outside his chest for you ... I am not going to be happy.'

Sometimes I forget that Mum is annoying but also bloody selfless. Could learn a thing or two about that.

She paused. 'Your dad would have understood.'

Millie started fidgeting in her baby seat. And then, the most extraordinary thing happened. Mum picked her up.

'Time for your bottle, baby?' she said to her gently.

Millie grabbed Mum's face in her chubby hand. It was the first time Mum had smiled since Moobs had left.

So weird how things can fall apart while others come together.

Wednesday 19th May

Have spent two weeks trying to get Mum to call her husband. Nothing. On plus side, Mum is looking after Millie when I work. Still haven't heard back from publisher about the job I applied for. Depressing.

*

Depression turned to anger at Sakeb because there's me, quietly walking away from the marriage – not wanting anything from him – not even what belongs to me! Because I felt guilty for leaving him for a baby. And he doesn't once call me and say, *Here, Sofe. Here's the money that we both saved. The money that is owed to you.*

Then I realised it's stupid to be angry about not getting something you didn't ask for. So, I did the adult thing and I wrote him a two-page email about him giving me my sodding half!

*

OMG I got an interview! Plus, Moobs called! I picked up and he asked to speak to Mum. I'm sorry but I had to have a go at him for not having called earlier (the email to Sakeb had lit a bit of an emotional fire, clearly). But he said he had been calling her every day for the past three weeks. She won't speak to him. Handed Mum the phone, but when I told her who it was, she hung up.

Oh dear.

Then she put Millie in the stroller and took her for a walk. Weird how this has come about, but maybe it's all part of God's bigger plan . . . We just don't know how it will end.

Conall messaged to ask whether Millie needed babysitting. Told him she's fixing Mum's heartbreak. He seemed to understand.

Friday 21st May

Job interview day! I've only been that nervous about three times in my life. It went fine, I think. But I couldn't stop sweating. I hope they don't think I'm always that sweaty. And that I'll actually be able to do the job . . .

Monday 24th May

Ugh. Been on phone to adoption agency for past hour and a half, asking what's happening with the papers. You'd think with so many babies needing a family, they'd hurry the hell up. Mum's out for a walk with Millie again. I still catch Mum looking sad, but then she goes and tells me to help her clean something. Yesterday it was the shed.

Can't sleep nowadays. Nothing from Sakeb.

Keep having fear that Millie will be taken away and that I'll end up living with Mum for ever.

Wednesday 26th May

Still nothing from Sakeb. Why, why *whyyyyy*? I remember the days waiting for a man to message after a date. Turns out they don't even bother messaging after a marriage, either.

Friday 28th May

Oh my God! Just got phone call about interview. I got the job! Not only that, but Sakeb responded to my email!

> Sofia,
>
> You are right. You are owed for the life we had. However much you disappointed me and the hope of us having a proper family, I see you're in urgent need of money. I have some savings that should help. We can talk about the rest of the money owed, and when and how I can get that to you.
>
> Let's not involve lawyers. I'm willing to be sensible if you are.
>
> Sakeb.

I mean, honestly. You'd think he was writing to an ex-colleague, not ex-wife. Also, I was an adult and ignored the dig about disappointment and lost hope for a 'proper' family, and the idea that I might not be a sensible person, because I was *too excited*.

Mum had just left to go to the shops and so I ran after her, Millie in my arms. When I told Mum both pieces of news she just looked at me.

'Okay.'

Which wasn't the excitement I'd expected.

'*Mum*. It means I can finally move out.'

The money from Sakeb, the new job, some money coming in from my freelancing . . . It all means I can *finally* be independent. Again. But her face went a little red. 'Yes, living with me must be very difficult with me cooking for you and looking after you and Amelia and doing everything for everyone.'

With which she marched away. I looked at her, confused, as she turned the corner. Then I realised that perhaps she thought I'd carry on living with her now Moobs had left.

Is it selfish to have stayed with her when I needed help, and then to leave her when she's on her own? Is it my fault her second marriage didn't work out? Bad enough she stayed in her first one because of the kids . . .

Oh dear, oh dear.

Turned to go back indoors when Conall came out.

'What's wrong with your face?' he asked.

'Where to start,' I said.

He gave a small laugh.

Then I told him about the job and that I'd

probably be moving out. I was hoping he'd look as upset as Mum clearly was.

'Good for you, Sofe,' he said.

I paused. 'No more neighbourly chats.'

He shook his head. I wanted to ask if he'd miss them. If he'd miss *me*. But that would've been stupid, since I'm trying not to miss him at all.

'Eamonn will be sad to see Amelia go,' said Conall.

I told him I'd bring her over to say goodbye.

How can trying to start afresh, which should be right, feel so wrong?

JUNE
Home and Away

Tuesday 1st June

Set a playdate with Foz and the girls. Took three
and a half hours to leave. Why does no one tell
you that being a mother means spending your
life packing things for baby and still forgetting
something? Went to The Rookery in Streatham,
where we both felt like we were in a romantic
film, until Foz's eldest pushed the youngest
into a bed of pink roses. I spent fifteen minutes
trying to calm the youngest while Foz gave the
eldest a telling-off.

'Was I too harsh?' she asked afterwards.

I wanted to say not harsh enough. But then
Millie spat up her milk.

'These girls drive me crazy,' Foz added.
Mummy, mummy, mummy. It's all I hear. Piss
off. Mummy wants a second to herself. The
other day, I was doing a poo and one of them
came in with her pants on her head, crying,
because she couldn't take them off.'

I laughed.

'That same day the other one ran straight

into a tree because she wanted to know how it would feel.'

'All the things I have to look forward to,' I said.

'Look at us,' replied Foz. 'Wouldn't you kill for a fag?'

'I'd sell the kids for a menthol.'

'You know it's a good idea to leave your mum's,' Foz said. 'I'm sure things will work out with her and whats-his-boob.'

'Isn't it like I'm deserting her?' I asked.

'You won't move far. And I don't think it's very healthy living next door to Conall. *Zara, stop feeding your sister worms! For God's sake . . .*'

Foz left and returned a few minutes later.

'It is comforting, though,' I said. 'Just knowing he's quite close.'

Foz shot me a look. 'He'll always be Conall . . . *the one*. I get it . . .'

'But?' I said.

Foz paused for a moment. 'There is no *but* actually. Nothing stays the same. Who knows? What's right this minute might not be right the next.'

'But we make our decisions based on the *now* not *what if*,' I replied.

'Exactly.'

And *now*, quite frankly, I needed to do

something on my own. Start living as a single mother like an actual adult.

Wednesday 16ᵗʰ June

Mum sees no point in me moving five streets away, but honestly, I think it's the best compromise. And I didn't even think about still being close to Conall. Obviously. I was moving boxes, and Mum was trying to get the removal man to give a discount, when Eamonn came out.

'Hello,' I said.

He paused.

'Here,' I added, handing him a box. 'You can help.'

He looked too confused to disagree or walk away.

'Good boy,' said Mum, patting him on the back, which I think just confused him more.

When all the boxes had been put away in the van, he just stood there.

'Thank you,' I said.

He shrugged.

Then he waited.

'Do you want to come inside? Lemonade? Or

do you like iced tea? Coffee? Or are you too young for that? When do kids start drinking caffeine? Although, you're not really a kid any more . . .'

God, I could talk a lot of shit sometimes.

He shook his head.

Eventually, he spoke.

'Can I . . .' he began. 'Can I come and see Mils some time?'

Mils. He had a nickname for her and honestly, in that moment, I could've hugged him.

'Of course,' I said.

He looked relieved. It was the second time I'd seen him smile.

'I always wanted a little brother or sister,' he added.

Before I could reply he walked away and back into his house.

Now I am finally in my own home. Though it doesn't feel like mine yet.

Monday 21st June

Argh! First day of new job and am running late. Millie up all night. Nanny (thanks to Sakeb, whose payment has helped me to find someone to look after the child he didn't want) got here an hour ago and keeps giving me a dirty look every time I leave a dish in the sink.

Rushed into the office building like mad woman. Spent all day trying to take in information about digital campaigns. All the while trying not to wonder about what the nanny was doing with Millie. Am an obsessive mother.

Oh dear.

*

Legged it home. Five missed calls from Mum. Kissed Millie a hundred times before demanding a minute-by-minute blow of what the nanny did with her all day. Did Millie like the chicken with her broccoli? How long did she nap? Did she say *mama* yet? Was she walking?

'I've been doing this for fifteen years,' said the nanny flatly.

'Oh, of course,' I replied.

Then I asked her about her poo. Millie's that is. Not the nanny's. Obviously.

So tired I don't have energy to call Mum back.

Friday 25th June

Have not had one minute. Not *one*. Spent work hours chasing the adoption company about the papers. On plus side, this means all I've thought about is getting through the day. And making sure Millie doesn't throw up every time she has chicken.

Shit. Still haven't called Mum back. Will go over tomorrow.

Sunday 27th June

Well, tomorrow didn't come. Bloody pipe burst in the kitchen. Mess everywhere. Millie crying because she didn't like the mashed carrots, and I didn't know where I'd put my phone. Couldn't get a plumber and so had to call Conall. He came with Eamonn. Millie jumped at seeing him. Eamonn looked very happy. As did Conall.

Love Conall's DIY skills. He's a fixer. Which can be a bad thing because I shouldn't get used to others fixing things for me. But I'm shit with pipes.

When he'd finished I told them to stay for dinner. Conall raised his eyebrows.

'*You're* going to cook?'

'No,' I replied. 'You're eating Millie's mashed carrots.'

Eamonn smiled. Again. He'd turn it into a habit if he wasn't careful. Ended up getting fish and chips from local chippy, sitting on sofa, while Conall told Eamonn about my kitchen skills.

'A house full of wedding guests,' he said, talking about the time my sister was getting married, 'and Sofe here drops an entire dish of biryani on her foot.'

I laughed. 'I limped for about three days.'

And for a moment, he caught my eye and held my gaze. I felt the battered cod rise to my throat. Maybe I used too much vinegar.

'They were good days,' he said, quietly.

Eamonn looked between us, and I wondered what it all meant, when the doorbell rang.

Mum was standing there. She looked relieved when I opened it.

'Oh, thanks to God. Why weren't you answering your phone?' she said, marching in.

She stopped when she saw Conall and

Eamonn, plates and ketchup spread over the coffee table.

There was a weird silence.

Mum looked at me. 'I have been calling you all week and you message that you are too busy, too tired to speak or see me, but look . . .'

She spread her arm towards the room.

'My pipe bur—'

She put her hand up. 'Always an excuse. When you need me you move in with me, and when you don't, you can't even ask me to come for dinner.'

She shot Conall a look. As if he were to blame. Which, I suppose if you looked at it in a certain way, he was.

'I—'

But before I could finish, she'd already stormed out of the house. I looked back at Conall, Eamonn and a gurgling Millie before I followed Mum.

'*Mum,*' I called out before I caught up with her.

When she turned around there were tears in her eyes and my heart sank to my ankles.

'"Even your children forget you," your dad would say,' said Mum.

It sounded more like something Mum would say. But, after them being married for forty years, maybe they caught each other's ideas as well as habits.

'I haven't forgotten you, Mum. I'm sorry, really, I ju—'

'Doesn't matter, Soffoo. Leave it.'

'Come over,' I said. 'Please.'

'No. I'm going home.'

'Are you okay?'

'Of course I'm not!'

You have to give credit to Punjabi parents for being honest.

'But it's not your problem,' she added.

Then I watched her walk away, back to her house, all alone.

*

When I returned, Conall told Eamonn to go home and that he'd follow.

'She okay?' he asked.

I shook my head. And then he brought me into his arms and hugged me, kissing the top of my head. I took in his scent. I've missed him holding me.

'It'll be okay,' he said.

I looked up at him. 'You're not very good at promising things.'

'I'm here,' he said. Then he paused before he added, 'I'll always be here.'

Monday 28th June

Conall
Tried knocking on your mum's door this morning. (She thought I was a delivery man.) Closed the door when she realised I wasn't.

Argh!! Conall's text message was followed by the nanny calling in sick. Bollocking bollocks.

I couldn't take the day off in my second week of work. Rang Mum but, when she didn't pick up, I had to grab Millie and her things in mad dash and went into the house (spare keys).

Mum was watching *Big Boss* – India's version of *Big Brother*.

'Mum, I know you're mad and you're right. I was really thoughtless but *please*, I need you to look after Millie. The nanny's sick and I have work.'

For a moment I must've looked so desperate that her face softened.

'Soffoo, I don't want to be those mothers who are passive *aggressive*, but sorry . . . no.'

'*No?*'

She pursed her lips. Then, firmly nodded. 'No.'

Perhaps it was wrong of me, but that pissed me off. Couldn't she see I needed help?

'Fine,' I said.

And without saying goodbye, I left the house and did the only other thing I could do. I knocked on Conall's door.

*

Spent all day at work unable to shake off being mad at Mum. And then, for some reason, I still felt guilty. All my life I've been so used to her saying yes to me when I've needed her, that I thought she'd always say yes. She didn't *owe* me childcare. And then, I remembered her words.

So when I marry a man that doesn't live with his heart outside his chest for you ... I am not going to be happy about it.

Got home and collected Millie. Conall invited me in. I was tired and wanted to go and see Mum, but also it was nice to see friendly faces. Even Eamonn cracked another smile.

'Sofe ...' Conall began, taking me by the hand. He led me into the kitchen, away from Millie and Eamonn.

My heart beat faster.

He was holding my hand.

'I don't want to do what I did last time

and not say anything,' he continued. 'Just stay silent, because I was too much of a coward.'

Funny, of all the things I thought of Conall, him being a coward was never one of them. To me, he had always been brave. You never do see yourself as others see you, I suppose.

'I don't know if there's a chance. If you'd ever forgive me. And even if you did, whether it would work because . . .'

He glanced outside the kitchen door where we could hear Eamonn talking to Millie about football.

'We've got responsibilities now. Things would be different, but I don't think that's a bad thing. But that's only if you could forgive me.' He paused.

My mouth was dry. A lump in my throat.

'Would you?'

'Conall,' I whispered.

I realised in that moment that I wanted him back. I always had. I just wanted *him* to do the trying.

And here he was, doing what I had secretly wanted.

'What about Eamonn?' I asked.

'I know.' He sighed. 'I know. I need to speak to him.'

'Don't you think you should've done that before you said all this to me?'

'Sofe, I just don't . . .'

'What? Don't what?'

'I just don't want to do life without you,' he said.

In the chaos of him saying all the things I had wanted to hear, the chance that we might be a family, that I might no longer be raising Millie alone, what did *I* want to do?

I wanted to talk to my mum.

JULY
Some Mothers Do Have 'Em

Friday 2nd July

I didn't care that she was angry with me, or that I was a little pissed off with her.

I left Conall's on Monday evening without saying anything. I told him I needed to think, but really, it was to get those organs in order. If my brain was in my chest and my heart in my head, then no good would come of anything.

I went straight to Mum's. She looked surprised to see me but then her face changed.

'Conall looked after Amelia today?' she asked.

She didn't even raise her voice like she usually does.

I nodded.

'Hmmm,' she replied.

I sat down, taking in the scent of Millie's hair. It was always a comfort. No matter how stressed I felt.

There was a long pause.

'Well?' she said.

I have always wondered whether my mum knows nothing or everything.

'He wants to get back together,' I answered.

She pursed her lips and paused *Big Boss* on the television. For a moment, I thought she might be pleased. She's been dying to marry me off since divorce number two and really, some might say that marrying my first husband would be less headache.

'I don't think it'll be like the first time,' I said. 'We're older. Wiser. I hope. We've both changed, learned our lessons and you know . . . realise that we've both got responsibilities.'

I bounced Millie on my knee.

It's always scary when Mum doesn't speak.

'Well? Don't you want to say something?' I asked. 'Don't you have thoughts?'

'What is the point in marrying the same man twice?' she said. 'He has a son who is moody. You know how difficult boys that age can be? And will he live with you until he goes to university? *If* he goes to university. I don't know if he is very bright.'

'Mum . . . He's so great with Millie.'

'Hmph. All men are a mistake, but you don't make the same one with the same man twice. That is *very* silly. Look at your age. Be sensible, Sofoo. You have always been too much romantic.'

Which I thought was a bit rich.

'*Mum*,' I said. '*Moobs* was *your* first love,' I reminded her.

'Shh,' she interrupted. 'We don't talk about those things.'

She unpaused the TV.

Mum spoke over the loud celebrities who were shouting over one another about some mess in the kitchen.

'You are a forty-year-old woman who is starting again from when she was thirty,' said Mum. 'Just *think*.'

After which she told me the show was getting very 'interested'.

That was my cue to leave.

Thursday 8th July

Bloody typical. The week Millie decides to sleep through the night, I can't bloody sleep at all. Have been awake thinking of the different ways me getting back with Conall could play out.

1. We both live happily ever after, never make the same mistakes twice, and *always*

tell each other what we are feeling. We will be able to read each other's minds.

Eamonn and Millie will become best friends. She will be so happy that she never thinks about her biological parents. He will be an adoring big brother and Conall's ex will never come back.

Mum and Moobs will get back together. We will all have Christmas at mine and Eid at Mum's. THERE ARE NO SECRETS. EVER.

2. It is a total disaster. We both realise that we made a mistake. Again. That we just *thought* we were still in love, but are not actually in love. (Although I believe this version less than I believe Conall's ex never coming back.)

Eamonn begins to hate Millie and Millie grows up traumatised. She needs therapy because she can never have a proper relationship with anyone. (She also spends her whole life looking for her biological parents, ends up finding them and leaving me and living with them for ever.) What is Christmas or Eid?

3. It is *very hard*. There are a hundred and one compromises to make. Eamonn will hate me, but I'll be patient and understanding

(losing my shit now and again), and one day he will like me. Though it might not happen until he is middle-aged and I no longer remember who he is.

Millie will have her ups and downs growing up. Eamonn might make it easier for her. Or harder. She will have questions when she's older. She will hurt. But we'll get through it.

Conall and I will need to have a million talks about what we will and will not do this time. That we won't hide things from one another.

Mum will take a while to get used to it. She will make digs at Conall, who will have to leave the room or go for a walk every time it happens. She and I will have more arguments. She and Moobs might never get back together.

Christmas and Eid will be difficult for the first few years. Maybe it always will be. There will be good days (which are the best) and bad days (where I wonder whether I should've just gone and lived in a cave). But. There will be love. And not only with Conall.

Tuesday 13th July

I've got the adoption papers. The actual papers! I go in at the end of the month to sign them and Millie will actually be mine. I will be responsible for her for the rest of my life. For her each and every sadness and happiness.

Don't know why I felt sick. This is what I'd been waiting for. I am happy, of course. It's just that when something has been a dream for so long, and it becomes a reality, it takes a while to adjust.

When I got the news there was only one person I wanted to tell.

Thursday 15th July

Went to Mum's to try and be a good daughter. But then gave her adoption news. She switched on *Big Boss* again.

Oh dear.

Sunday 18th July

Spent day with Foz and kids in the park. Told her what happened with Conall and weird feeling about adoption.

Her response was: 'Life, eh.'

I nodded as we blinked our eyes against the sun, watching the girls playing. Millie was gurgling on the blanket. Foz and I stuffing our faces with Pret sandwiches and drinks.

'In the end it's just going to be you and me, anyway,' I said.

'Exactly, darling. Just another, what? Eighteen years?'

'Unless they all turn out to be geniuses,' I added.

At that point, Foz's youngest banged her head against a tree trunk.

Foz shook her head. 'I'll be grateful if they're just happy and healthy.'

And that, of course, was all anyone could wish for.

Friday 30th July

Would've liked Mum to come along for adoption finalising, but she was obviously watching *Big Boss*. Conall knocked on my door at eight in the morning.

'I'm coming with you,' he said.

We both ignored the conversation we'd had. Maybe he hadn't talked to Eamonn. Maybe I should've said that I wanted him back. Of course I did. But it all felt confusing. And then anyway, there were other things happening. He tried to keep me talking as we walked into the building. I don't know why I felt so nervous. As if something was about to go wrong.

We walked into the waiting room and I felt my heart in my throat. (Obviously I have organ displacement disorder.)

As soon as the social worker came out, I knew something wasn't right.

'Sofia . . .' she said, shaking my hand.

'What's wrong?' I asked.

She gave a tight smile. 'Let's go into the office.'

She looked at Conall, who had already grabbed my hand.

'There's been a slight problem,' she said, as we all sat down.

Now my heart was in my knees.

'What problem?' I asked.

Millie gurgled.

The social worker paused. 'Amelia's mother contacted us this morning.'

I waited.

'She wants to see Amelia.'

'What does that mean?' I asked. 'Where are the papers?'

'I'll be honest. It means she's having doubts. She's not signing the papers until she's seen Amelia.'

'But what will that *do*?' I said.

I had to calm my voice.

Conall spoke. 'What'll happen next?'

'We'll arrange a date for Amelia's mum to see her. Supervised, of course, and we'll have to assess things from there.'

'What things?' I asked.

She sighed and gave a sympathetic smile. 'There's always a risk like this when it comes to adopting.'

'What risk?' I pressed, even though I knew.

Of course I knew. I just needed to hear it.

'That the mother will want her baby back.'

AUGUST
Cry, Baby

Sunday 1ˢᵗ August

Would stay in bed all day if I didn't have a baby. Did I bring this on myself? When I got the adoption papers more than two weeks ago now, I had been relieved but also nervous.

Conall told me I was being ridiculous. That I had always known the risks before I started the process.

Keep staring at Millie and wondering what life would be like without her. Which is when I feel a stab in my chest. Have urge to go and tell Mum what's going on. Don't know why. She'll probably be over the moon. But still. A person needs their mother.

*

Went over (she was watching TV, of course). There were dishes in the sink. Dust on the cabinets. Empty food wrappers on the coffee table.

'*Mum*,' I said, walking into the living room.

She looked up at me, surprised. 'I didn't hear the door open.'

I looked around at the mess. Then I settled Millie down, went into the kitchen to get the rubber gloves, and started cleaning the house.

Mum told me to leave everything. She'd do it later. She only said this once before she got back to the television. When I'd come downstairs after cleaning the bathroom (must hire Mum a cleaner) she was still on the sofa. Only this time, Millie was next to her. She was chewing on her own hand (Millie, not Mum) while Mum was telling her what was happening on the screen.

Felt my heart break a little. Why couldn't this have happened sooner? Before I might have lost Millie.

I took the remote, switched off the TV and pulled up a chair in front of Mum.

Then, making sure she was listening to me, I told her how Millie might no longer be mine.

Mum simply took Millie in her lap and switched the TV back on.

Thursday 5th August

Conall has either been coming over or calling every day. Beginning to wonder why I am confused about getting back with him.

Monday 16th August

It was the first visit with Millie's biological mum, Sarah. We met with the social worker in a local park. I left work early for the meeting. When I saw how nervous Sarah looked, I felt sorry for her. I went towards my car, looking back as she took Millie from the social worker. She looked scared, as if she might drop her.

Sarah was about twenty-eight, but she had come from a troubled family and when she got pregnant out of wedlock, they disowned her. Millie's dad was nowhere to be seen. Sarah suffered from depression, was alone, with no help and didn't feel she could look after a baby. Before I had handed Millie to the social worker, I felt jealous. What if they had that mother–daughter bond and Millie didn't want to come back to me?

I got to my car and saw that Millie looked like she was about to cry. Sarah was handing her back to the social worker. Sarah also looked like she was about to cry. Even though she was twenty-eight she seemed so young, not sure where she was or where she belonged.

I rushed over from the car.

'Don't worry,' I said to Sarah. 'She'll get used to you.'

She looked relieved.

I was about to leave again when she spoke. 'Thank you.'

I turned around.

'For taking care of her so well,' Sarah added.

I couldn't quite bring myself to say that actually it was Millie that took care of me.

The social worker brought Millie back a few hours later.

'How was it?' I asked her nervously, taking Millie and hugging her.

'Fine.' She paused. 'She wants to see her again.'

My heart sank.

'What does that mean?' I asked.

The social worker gave me a sympathetic smile. 'I had a long conversation with Sarah, and all she wants is to see Millie. She knows that you will give her a better life than she ever could.'

I should've been glad. But it only made me feel more depressed.

No mother should have to feel that way.

Friday 27ᵗʰ August

Sarah has Millie for a whole afternoon today. I had taken the day off work because I couldn't concentrate. Went to Mum's and she switched *Big Boss* off. Then she made me spag bol (Pakistani style) because it's always been my comfort food.

We both ate in silence.

After a while I spoke. 'Is it wrong that sometimes I wonder what life would've been like without Millie?'

'*Of course not*,' she said. 'Life without children is easier. But that doesn't mean it's better. Look at Millie's mother,' Mum continued. 'Her life might be easier without Millie, but she knows it's not better.'

And before Mum added some more cheese to her spag bol, she finally said, 'A life without your child never can be.'

SEPTEMBER

Third Time Lucky. Again.

Friday 3rd September

Conall's invited me over for dinner, which is rather formal. We usually just pop into each other's homes, but there's never been a dinner *invitation*. It's making me nervous. I've changed my outfit about a million times, until Mum just came in and told me I could go in a bin bag and he still wouldn't mind.

Has Mum become . . . *a friend*?

She just came into my room again and told me the green dress makes the bags under my eyes worse.

Lovely.

*

Oh, God. What has just happened? Eamonn opened the door and said hello to me. Actual hello, with a sort of smile. I mean, at least he tried. He looked disappointed when I told him Mum was looking after Millie.

I swear I love that boy just for how much he loves my daughter.

Conall was in the kitchen and called out for

me to take a seat in the dining room. The table was laid out beautifully. Candles in the centre and little flowers on each plate.

'Did your dad do this?' I whispered to Eamonn.

Conall's sense of romance *never* involved flowers.

He shook his head and mumbled something.

'Sorry,' I said, leaning forward to try to hear him better.

'It was me.'

'Oh,' I said.

He just shrugged and went a deep shade of red.

'It's lovely,' I added.

I realised that maybe Eamonn was a bit of a romantic. Conall came in wearing jeans and a white shirt and I felt my heart skip a beat.

'You look nice,' he said.

'I managed a shower today.'

'Thought I smelt a lack of fried onions,' replied Conall.

'Racist.'

He laughed. I laughed. Eamonn looked uncomfortable.

I was told to sit at the table as Eamonn brought in a salad and breads with cheese (who doesn't like cheese?) followed by Conall with lasagne.

'I figured I'd keep it simple,' he said.

The table flickered with candlelight, cutlery clinked. I asked Eamonn how school was, whether he'd made friends. All the boring questions that I'm sure I hated when I was his age.

As the evening passed, Eamonn seemed more and more relaxed. He'd look at Conall every few minutes as if worried. Not sure why.

Conall kept dropping his fork, pouring too much drink in the glasses. Once or twice I caught him looking at me. I felt my face flush, as if I was sixteen again. Ah, youth! Imagine when I had all that time to make mistakes, get over them and then start again. There was no room for mistakes any more, especially not when there were children involved.

'I'm a bit nervous about Millie's mum,' I said, when Conall asked how she was.

Eamonn looked up.

'It's got to be tough,' said Conall.

I had been trying not to think about it all evening (for once) but I'd suddenly lost my appetite.

'You might lose her?' asked Eamonn.

'Let's not talk about it right now, shall we?' replied Conall, giving Eamonn a look. 'Listen, Sofe, the reason I ... *we*, called you over ...'

He cleared his throat. Took a deep breath. 'I've told Eamonn that I've spoken to you about possibly getting back together.'

I choked on a crust of bread. Eamonn was looking at the tablecloth.

'I know it's not going to be easy. I know there's a lot going on, but I also think . . . at our time in life, we can't be scared to do the things we want. No matter how hard it might be.'

I wanted to cry. Actually cry.

'Eamonn . . .' I said, leaning towards him. 'Are you okay with this?'

He looked me in the eye and I'm not sure what it meant. He just shrugged.

'Fine,' he said, eventually.

And I realised I had been waiting for his approval. Any doubts I had just disappeared. For a moment, it felt as if nothing in the world could go wrong. Moobs would come back. Mum would be happy. I'd move in here. Millie would be mine. Foz's girls would grow up too and stop hitting their heads against trees. *Everything would be fine.*

'Are we really doing this?' I asked.

Conall nodded. 'I know we need to figure out what's happening with Millie. But, God, yes. Let's do this.'

He didn't move from his seat. Nor did I.

'Okay then. Well, I suppose that's that. Is there dessert?' I asked with a smile.

And this time when we carried on speaking, we talked about when we'd get married (ASAP), where (London), who we'd invite (about ten people) and where I would live. (Here. Obviously.)

When we were at the door alone, saying goodbye, Conall got out a ring from his jeans pocket.

'Can't have people thinking you're single now,' he said, laughing.

'That's a shame,' I replied. 'You see the queue out there, don't you? So many choices.'

He shook his head, brought me closer to him and whispered, 'There was only ever one choice.'

God, I love him.

Saturday 4th September

Had head in clouds for about five minutes before I told Mum. She started stomping around, telling me what a mistake I'm making. Then she stopped.

'Now. What clothes shall I have made for you from Pakistan?'

Also, wondering if I have to tell adoption agency. Will it take longer to get the papers signed? Hmmm. Had not considered this before.

Thursday 9th September

Oh, Lord! Mum has already told all our relatives that I'm getting married again to husband number one. I don't understand how she can be so against a marriage, and then want to organise the whole thing. At least it's keeping her busy.

Friday 17th September

Millie's seeing Sarah again today. I spoke to adoption agency about my engagement. Now there will be interviews and all sorts and *argh*.

But, must remember the best things in life are never easy . . .

Thursday 30ᵗʰ September

Bloody, bloody hell. Mum keeps asking me what date the wedding will be, because don't I know how long it takes to have a wedding outfit made. There have been weeks of interviews and social workers, visiting Conall and speaking to him and Eamonn. Every time there's another visit my heart is in my mouth. But must keep faith that all will be fine.

Another visit with Sarah tomorrow. This time without supervision. Must remember that soon it will be over. Sarah can be a part of her life, but in the end Millie has to be mine, because I know I can care for her better. And doesn't she deserve the best type of life? Not one of tension with a mother who isn't stable.

Yet, every now and then, Mum's words rattle around in my brain: *A life without your child can never be better.*

OCTOBER
Sweet Child of Mine

Friday 1st October

Sarah almost couldn't seem to hand Millie over to me today. I invited her inside the house. She looked around. The bookshelves. The pictures of Millie and me. Of my friends and family.

'You have a lot of people in your life,' she said.

I made us both some tea.

'Look at all those toys,' she added.

For a moment, I felt guilty. Life, though obviously not easy (working class, Pakistani, second generation immigrant, etc., etc.) had clearly been easier for me than it had been for Sarah. She looked at Millie in her playpen.

'She's happy here.'

'I hope so,' I replied. 'Everything is about her, you know?'

Then I went into the story about how fostering Millie had meant a divorce from my second husband. So, everything *had* to be about Millie. Otherwise what would have been the point? Although, now, looking back, all of that had led me to *this* point. Getting back with

Conall – everything seemed to come together. I was suddenly very grateful for a husband who didn't want to adopt.

'I know it must be hard for you,' I said.

She gave a strained smile. 'Some people have more choices than others. That's just the way it is.'

I know the social worker said that Sarah didn't want to take Millie away, but sometimes, in the middle of the night, I'd wake up with this *knowledge* that she'd no longer be mine. Sarah spoke, as if reading my thoughts.

'I just like seeing her. How she's doing.'

'Of course,' I replied.

'That she's safe,' said Sarah.

'I promise she is.'

She nodded. 'I can tell. And you know, I wouldn't take that away from her.'

Her voice cracked and there were tears in her eyes. I went and sat next to her.

'I'm just so grateful that she has you,' she said.

But instead of feeling relieved that she wouldn't want Millie back, I felt guilty. As if me wanting Millie was wrong. And by wanting her, I was stopping Sarah from having what *she* wanted.

'You'll *always* be able to see her,' I said. 'And

I'll always be honest about who her biological mother is.'

Sarah simply smiled and wiped away her tears.

*

When she left, I put Millie to bed and ended up staying awake for hours, staring at her, asking myself the same question: *who does Millie really belong to?*

I didn't find an answer.

Saturday 9ᵗʰ October

I can't take it any more. I've prayed for patience. I've tried to remember the importance of mothers in Islam, but I can't take it any more. *I am sorry, God.*

Mum barged into the flat today. I was making up Millie's bottle in the kitchen when Mum started measuring the width of my hips with a tape.

'Hmmm. You have lost weight.'

'What are you doing?' I asked.

'*Your clothes,* Sofoo.'

'It's my *third* wedding,' I replied. 'We're just going to get our favourite people and go to the mosque, Mum.'

Then, I realised (always too late when it comes to my mother) that she still misses Moobs. And the wedding means she doesn't have to think about how much she is missing him. I mean, at least she's not spending all day watching repeats of *Big Boss*.

'Okay, Mum,' I said. 'Whatever you want.'

So, she whipped out the tape again and started measuring my boobs.

Sunday 10th October

I hadn't tried hard enough. That was the problem. With Moobs. I called him once and then just left it. What if I tried just the once with everything in life? I'd be a single forty-year-old, living with my mother, I'm pretty sure. So, it was time for some detective work.

I called Mum's bestie, who knew Moobs' cousin's aunt's daughter. She knew Moobs' high school friend who lives in Scotland now.

Which is where Moobs had been staying for a while. He'd been moving around apparently. From family member to family member.

What if he went back to Pakistan?

What if he thought Mum didn't care about him?

What if I ruined her only chance of happiness?

Thankfully, it turned out he was now staying with a cousin in East London. So, I left Millie with Conall and Eamonn, and drove up there. I banged on the door. I was feeling very spirited.

'Salam,' I said to the auntie who'd answered the door. 'Is Moob— I mean, Uncle Mehboob home?'

Eventually she let me in.

'We are always happy to have guests,' she said, as she sat me down in the living room. 'But you know how people talk. What will he do with his life?'

Oh dear. So I guess being single in your 70s means having to hear the same question too.

After about ten minutes of awkward conversation, Moobs walked in. He looked at me and gave a loud laugh, smiled, shook my hand as if we were work colleagues. The aunt looked at him, confused.

'Now you are seeing him like this. Earlier

he was crying into a ladoo. Those sweetmeats always have been his favourite.'

With which she left the room. Moobs looked embarrassed.

'I know I am a man. But we do have feelings,' he said.

I leaned forward and patted him on his hand. Weird being the go-between in my mum's love life, with a man who isn't my father. But we live and learn that not everything happens the way one thinks it will.

'She misses you,' I said.

He looked up at me, his bald head made shinier in his excitement. The look went as fast as it had come.

'If she missed me, she would've answered my phone calls. She wouldn't make me do something I—' He stopped. 'Sorry, but I didn't feel it was right.'

I waved my hand. 'Oh, don't worry about that. She's over that. She knows that me marrying your nephew wasn't right. You know how Mum panics.'

He smiled as if remembering something. 'Why do you think I keep the kitchen so full?'

I felt a rush of affection for Moobs.

'Is this how you want to live?' I said. 'Going from one cousin's home to the next? Isn't it time that you should be settled and . . . happy?'

He nodded.

'Even if you don't say you're sorry. Even if you just tell her not being with her is the worst thing there is – she'll be fine.'

'Really?' he asked, looking hopeful.

'I promise.' Then I paused before I added, 'It's time for you to come home.'

Friday 22nd October

Hurrah! I'm a matchmaking genius! Moobs came back and, in true Romeo fashion, knocked on the door and said, 'Next time I will help you look for a nice boy for Sofia.'

Mum then filled him in that he doesn't have to worry about that. Conall and Eamonn came to Mum's for dinner and everyone was in an excellent mood. Millie was passed from person to person, but she didn't want to go to anyone except Eamonn. Who says life can't work out if you're twice divorced?

When everyone left and I had gone back home, leaving Moobs and Mum to have their . . . oh dear . . . reunion, I looked at Millie. She was falling asleep in her cot. An anxiety rose in my chest again but I pushed it back. If Sarah wants me to be Millie's mother then who am I to say no?

Why go and ruin something that is going perfectly well?

NOVEMBER
Nobody Said it was Easy

Tuesday 2nd November

Argh! Mum keeps calling me at work and giving me new names to put on the wedding guest list. *Why is it so long?*

'*Mum,*' I hissed into the phone so the assistant didn't hear me. 'There are ten people coming to the mosque and then forty for the evening dinner. That's what me and Conall planned.'

Quiet.

'Hello?'

More quiet.

'So, what will I say to Auntie Nargis and her sister who is visiting?'

God, please help me. 'Ask if they really want to give me a gift for the third time when it might not work out?'

'*Soffoo,*' said Mum. 'Don't say things like this. We always hope for the best. But you are quite difficult.'

'Bye, Mum.'

*

Have been umming and ahing about inviting Sarah to the wedding. Conall thinks it might be weird for her. But wouldn't it be rude to *not* invite her? I see her now every week and we end up spending hours just chatting about Millie and other things. If she doesn't want to come then she doesn't have to. I'll say it's entirely up to her.

I think this is sensible.

Friday 5th November

Sarah brought Millie back later than usual. I was getting worried, calling her phone. I was about to call the social worker when she showed up at the door an hour late. I was obviously annoyed. The least she could've done was let me know.

Then I saw her face. She looked upset.

'Are you okay?' I asked, about to take Millie from her.

Instead, Sarah walked into the living room with my baby still in her arms.

'I lost track of the time,' she said.

But her words sounded distant. Millie reached

out to me but Sarah still didn't give her over. My heart began to thud faster than usual.

Then Sarah looked at me. 'How do things just work out for people like you?'

'Sorry?'

'Look at this place.'

Which was weird because it was a two-bedroom flat in Tooting.

'All these *things*,' she added.

I've never looked at my life as if it might be something that someone would actually *want*. Who would want two failed marriages? I know that Conall and I are getting married again, and I am happy, of course. But it's not going to be without its problems. Who knows when his ex will turn up and demand God knows what? Who knows if Eamonn will continue to like me when I'm living with him and his dad?

'How is it that two people,' Sarah went on, 'can have such different lives? Does it seem fair to you?'

I shook my head.

She paused for a few moments before giving Millie back. 'I'm sorry. It's just a bad day and . . .' She looked at Millie and broke out into a smile. 'We had such a great time today, didn't we, Mimi?'

'Mimi?' I asked.

'Sorry. My nickname for her.'

She took her little hand. Millie grabbed Sarah's finger.

'I know I'm doing the right thing for her,' said Sarah, eventually. 'But I can't do *this* any more. Pretend we're friends when you're the woman who has my baby because I can't be a proper mother.'

I wanted to say that of course she could – but what would that have meant?

'I can't pretend it doesn't kill me every time I leave her here with you instead of taking her home. Do you know what it's like to be all alone? To have no family support because you had a baby out of wedlock? To be thrown out of your home? I don't have any sisters. My younger brother calls me and even then he only talks for five minutes in case he's caught.'

'Sarah . . . I'm so sorry.'

'And I'm giving up the *one* thing that would at least give me some hope . . . and isn't hope the thing that life's meant to be about?'

I didn't know what to say. Or how to feel.

'I want her to have the best chance at life,' said Sarah. 'And you're going to do that, aren't you?'

'Of course,' I replied, though it came out so low I wonder if she heard.

'That's all I need to know . . . because the

rest of this. Every week? It's too much. I can't take it.'

I held on to Millie as if Sarah would snatch her from me and run out of the door. And the only thing I was left wondering when Sarah left (without Millie) is: didn't she have every right to?

Sunday 7th November

Haven't stopped thinking about Sarah. I told Conall what happened.

'Poor woman,' he said. 'That's such a shit situation.'

I nodded.

He brought me tea.

'What are you going to do?' he asked.

'*Do?*'

There was a long pause.

'What can I do?' I said, eventually.

Silence.

'I'm open to Sarah being a part of Millie's life,' I said. 'She can take her once a week, play with her. It's not ideal, but if it's good for Millie, then that's what counts.'

More silence. So, of course, I carried on.

'What else am I meant to do? What other options are there? None. That's the thing. Sarah doesn't want to be a part of Millie's life and there's nothing I can do about that.'

I carried on like this for several minutes before I ran out of steam because I was just repeating myself.

'There is something you can do,' said Conall.

My mouth felt dry. I was finding it hard to swallow.

'And what's that?' I asked.

Although I felt my chest heavy with something. The burden of knowledge.

Conall put his hand over mine, kissed me on my forehead and said, 'I think you know.'

*

Dinner at Mum's. Moobs had convinced Eamonn to play Scrabble, so he was forced to put his phone away.

Ugh. Hate it when someone says something that you knew all along. When I fostered Millie, it was because I thought I was doing a good thing. Helping someone. Giving back to the world, etc. But if that was really true, then I wouldn't be hanging on to her like this. Even good deeds can end up being selfish.

Mum was showing me Pakistani outfits of hers, dating back more than a few decades. She brought out her wedding dress.

'Look at this material. So in fashion now,' she said.

I touched the embroidery.

'If you were me, would you give Millie back to her mum?' I asked quietly.

Mum paused. She folded her old wedding dress carefully.

'I wouldn't have had Millie in the first place,' she said, after a while.

'Yes, thanks, Mum. Helpful.'

She shrugged. 'Things were different. I didn't even think not to have my own children and instead raise someone else's. But then you are different.'

She made a face as if she'd smelt rotten fish.

'Just a simple answer would do, Mum.'

'You have spent all this time looking after her, raising her, spending money on her. *Worrying* about her. Oof . . .'

She went on like this for some time.

'And . . . ?' I asked eventually.

'And still,' said Mum, sighing. 'If Sarah had not come back. If Millie had no one else, then maybe it would be different.'

'Mum . . .'

I wanted to cry.

'Sorry, Soffoo. No matter what you want or what you say . . . A mother is a mother.'

Saturday 13th November

Spoke to Conall who obviously thinks it's the right thing to do. Telling Eamonn tonight. Bet he's going to be thrilled. I've taken some time off work. Just to spend extra time with Millie. Taking photos of her. Making as many memories as I can before I . . . I can't even bring myself to write it.

But I can't pretend to have tried to do some good, only to then not do the one good thing I can do right now. Step aside and help a mother be with her baby.

*

Oh my God. What drama! I'm still so confused and . . . that can't actually have happened. Conall and I wanted to tell Eamonn together about me giving Millie back to Sarah. I don't know how Sarah will react when I tell her, but I hope

138

that she will still let me be a part of Millie's life. And I'm going to help her, however I can. Financially, looking after Millie, that kind of thing.

Am I happy about it? No. Is it the right thing to do?

Yes.

Unfortunately.

Anyway, we sat at the dinner table and I was trying to steady my voice (because every time I think about what I have to do I start crying). So, I just came out with it.

'Millie's going back to her mum.'

Then I ate a Yorkshire pudding. Just to put something in my mouth, you know? Eamonn looked from me to his dad. From his dad to me. From me to his dad. This went on for the entire time I chewed the Yorkshire pudding.

Then, out of nowhere (or I suppose somewhere) Eamonn just flings his cutlery on the plate, pushes his chair back (that falls down) and shouts, 'I'm fed up of this shit. Of everything changing. And no one ever asking me what *I* want.'

'Eamonn, calm down,' said Conall, also standing up. 'Pick up the chair, sit down and we'll talk about this.'

'Why?' shouted Eamonn. 'What's the point when no one gives a shit what I say.'

I began: 'That's not t—'

'Oh, just shut up.'

Eamonn said it with such hatred, even I was surprised. He looked at me like I was the one who had abandoned him as a child, not Conall.

'*Eamonn*,' said Conall.

'You're going to take her side again? As usual. Who the fuck is she? There was *one* good thing about her. About just *being* here and that's gone. She's just giving Millie up. Like that?'

'I'm not giving her—'

'Now you're getting your husband back no one else matters. I see how that goes.'

'Eamonn,' spoke Conall. His voice measured. 'I said, sit the fuck down.'

Oh dear.

'You marry her,' said Eamonn, already walking out of the room.

Conall grabbed his arm. '*Sit down*.'

'You can't tell me to do shit,' replied Eamonn. 'Not any more. You *promised* it was just going to be you and me. And then *she* came along. And it wasn't so bad with the baby. But *this*?'

With which he stormed out of the room, slamming the door behind him. Conall was standing, his hand on his forehead.

'Jesus, Sofe, I'm sorry.'

'Guess he doesn't like me as much without Millie.'

What was I without her? *Who* was I without her?

I waited for Conall to tell me I was wrong. That Eamonn would come round.

'Maybe I should go,' I said.

Never say a thing when you want the opposite answer. I mean, after forty years of life, you'd think I'd learned that much.

'Maybe it's best for now,' Conall replied.

And that's when I knew.

I'd lost everything. Again.

Friday 19th November

When I told Mum that I was going to give Millie back to her mother, I wasn't expecting her to look sad. Even though she did say, 'Your life will be easier for it.'

I chose not to tell her that since my decision, Conall and I have hardly spoken. He says he needs time to figure things out with Eamonn, but honestly, what is there to figure out? Who can deal with so much drama in their life?

I can't even move back in with Mum now Moobs is back.

I will die alone.

But then, there are worse things in life. I've heard.

Sarah had said she was never going to see Millie again, so I spoke to the social worker about providing Sarah with financial help. Supporting her with Millie. Being a guardian for Millie. We arranged to go and see her. Sarah looked so confused the whole time. And all I felt was heartbreak.

'We'll want to make the transfer as comfortable for Amelia as possible,' said the social worker.

I held on to Millie and wondered what the hell I was doing. But, it just didn't feel like there was any other choice. That's the thing when something is right – no matter how much you hate it.

As we left – Millie still with me – Sarah stopped me at the door.

'Why are you doing this?' she asked.

I shrugged. 'If I didn't, I think I'd feel bad for the rest of my life. It's selfish in that sense,' I added.

Then, Sarah pulled me into a hug and whispered in my ear: 'Thank you, thank you, thank you.'

Sunday 21st November

'Listen, you're going to have to tell me what's going on sooner or later and really I'd prefer sooner,' I said when Conall answered his door.

I'd had enough. Pretending everything was okay. That the answer would come to me when he was ready.

I am too old for that shit.

He let me in.

'I'm not just waiting around any more,' I added.

He rubbed his forehead.

'Sofe, I—'

I put my hand up. 'Okay.'

He looked at me.

'It's not going to work, right?' I said.

'No, it's just tha—'

'You have other responsibilities,' I interrupted. 'You need to put Eamonn first. You have to be the father you weren't when he was growing up ... etc. etc.'

'Sofe ...'

For a moment I couldn't speak. Something caught in my throat. Life. Love. Whatever you want to call it.

It snagged.

'I didn't know the same person could disappoint you twice,' I said.

'That's not fair,' he replied.

'But it's true, isn't it? The only difference is this time it was my fault for thinking things would be different.'

'I wish—'

'No,' I interrupted again. I shook my head. 'Grown-ups don't wish for things, Conall. They just fucking do them.'

I don't know why, but in that moment I felt more solid than I ever have done. How can that be when you've lost so many things in such a short space of time? Then I looked at his face which seemed so sad and lost. I put my hand on his cheek, brought him closer to me, and kissed him.

When I left his house, I had to steady my breathing, but couldn't stop my hands from shaking. And there was only one place I wanted to be.

144

I walked into Mum's house, into the kitchen where she was cooking. I burst into tears and she hugged me, letting the lamb biryani on the hob burn dry.

Saturday 27th November

Mum came over and spent the day helping me get all of Millie's things together. Felt slow and sad. Millie didn't whine or moan. She just smacked the table and laughed when I pretended to sneeze. The whole house has been full of her. My life has been full of her, and I don't know what I'm meant to do with myself after her.

And all of this was just made worse because she will never know how much she's meant to me. How she got me through each dark day. Her being a magnet for happiness. She will forget me, but I will never forget her and maybe that is what love is. Holding on to it, even when it doesn't hold on to you.

Sarah came and left with my baby. Mum stayed with me until I'd cried myself to sleep.

DECEMBER
Silent Nights

Wednesday 1st December

Why did I even bother getting a job? It just means having to get dressed in the morning. Although today I went into the office and went to use the loo. Pulled my jeans down and was wearing two pairs of knickers.

Bet I'll go home today and will have run out of pants.

Thursday 2nd December

Came home today and ordered two pizzas. They were on a two-for-one offer which sounded just about right given I lost two for one.

Didn't end up eating anything. Just stared at the boxes until I fell asleep on sofa.

Friday 3rd December

Argh! Woke up to pizza plastered to my face. Was late for work. Kept looking at photos of Millie on my phone. Then came across the one where she's playing with bloody Eamonn, and Conall is looking at both of them and smiling. Cried at desk.

Tomorrow I will stop feeling sorry for myself.

Saturday 4th December

'The good thing about the break-up this time,' said Foz, 'is that at least you know you've got over it before.'

She had managed to leave the children with her husband and was clearly enjoying a rare two-hour window without kids. She'd put her feet up on my coffee table and was eating a big packet of crisps.

'And I know it's more to do with Millie but . . .' She sat up. 'You did the right thing.'

'So everyone keeps telling me. But can I just

add that if I had done the wrong thing, then I'd still be marrying Conall. And I'd have a baby.'

Foz nodded. 'Yeah, that's a bit shit really.'

We sat for the rest of the afternoon eating crisps from the packet and drinking Coke from the bottle. We were a packet of fags short of being at university again.

Then there was banging at the door.

I managed to pull myself off the sofa, only for Mum to barge in and start cleaning the room.

'Fozia,' Mum exclaimed. 'You should know better. You have three children. You should be telling her that life is still worth living. Look at me. Seventy years old and did I give up?'

'No, Auntie,' said Fozia, beginning to help Mum with the cleaning up. 'But, to be fair, I don't think Sofe has given up . . .'

And then it struck me that I was acting as if I *had* given up. What had feeling sorry for myself ever achieved? What good would it do me? At some point in the near future, I would have to think about what my life *meant*, but in the meantime I felt *angry*.

Angry that all it took was *one* glitch and Conall gave in to Eamonn. He didn't even try. Because he was too scared and honestly, didn't he know that being a parent was just about being scared *all the time*. But that it didn't mean having to stop living your own life too. All he was doing was setting Eamonn up for disappointment whenever he didn't get what he wanted.

'No,' I said, eventually. 'I've *not* given up.'

With that I marched out of the house and to Conall's. I banged on his door. Finally, Eamonn opened it.

'Ugh,' he said, as he tried to close the door in my face.

I stopped it with my foot.

'You know,' I started. 'You have every right to be angry with your dad. Trust me, no one's more pissed with him than me.'

Eamonn went to turn away as I saw Conall coming down the stairs.

'But I'm not the one that left you,' I said. '*He* did. And he spent most of our marriage feeling so guilty it broke us.'

Eamonn turned to go into the living room, but I blocked his way.

'There are only so many ways he can say sorry. But if you think stopping him from marrying me is somehow going to prove that he loves you more than anything—'

And that was the moment. The realisation that Conall will never love me more than he loves Eamonn. That this kid will always come first.

Eamonn looked at me, as if waiting for the rest. But I wasn't quite sure where to go from there.

'Then you're right,' I said, finally.

Eamonn's shoulders seemed to relax. Unlike his frown.

'No one else will ever even come close,' I added. 'Every decision he's going to make, he's going to think of whether it's good for you – forget what *he* wants . . . or *needs*.'

I glanced at Conall, still halfway down the stairs, staring at me.

'And I'm okay with that,' I added. 'That's how it should be. But I am not okay with you making his life shit just so you can get some sort of revenge.'

Eamonn looked at the floor. I heard him mumble.

'What?' I said, leaning forward.

'I said it's your fault they're not together. If he didn't care about you, he would've got back with my mum and I wouldn't have to live two different lives.'

Conall came down the stairs. 'Eams. You don't think that's true, do you?'

When Eamonn looked up, there were tears

in his eyes. Perhaps I should've held back on the shouting.

'I'm sorry,' Conall told Eamonn. 'But even if I did want that, which I don't,' he added quickly, looking at me. 'But even if I did. Your mother would never want me back. We were all wrong for each other.'

'Not wrong enough to have me,' said Eamonn, wiping his eyes.

'Well, you have to do a few things right in life,' said Conall.

And then he brought Eamonn into a hug. He looked at me and mouthed *thank you*.

Which was the right time for me to leave.

Monday 6ᵗʰ December

Managed to only cry twice at desk today. I think that's an improvement. Sarah called to organise my visit to Millie.

Also, have started to look into fostering again. If at once you don't succeed . . .

Wednesday 8th December

Mum and Moobs are having the kitchen redone. Had gone over after work to help them (because what else am I doing with my life?).

'There was a lot of shouting next door,' said Moobs, as I packed the glasses away.

Mum shot him a look. 'It's none of our business.'

Ha!

'What was the shouting about?' I asked.

'Oh, mostly it was just Eamonn,' he replied. 'If he was my child, I would have slapped him a few times.'

Charming. There are some positives to the modern world, I suppose.

'Here, take these plates,' said Mum, pushing the dishes into Moobs' hands, telling him to box them up in the conservatory.

'Doesn't matter what they're shouting about,' added Mum after a few minutes. 'You just carry on helping us with the kitchen.'

So, that's what I did.

Sunday 12th December

Oh my actual God. After days of helping Mum and Moobs with the kitchen and with no other responsibilities, I spent entire morning in my pyjamas, watching crappy television and eating whatever I could find in the fridge (half an avocado, one mini pancake, a bowl of Cornflakes with honey, a slice of toast with cheese that I think's been in the fridge since I moved in).

The doorbell rang. I swear, if it was Mum, I'd have to slam the door in her face because it was Sunday and surely I deserved *one* more day of moping. But it wasn't Mum.

'Oh,' I said, opening the door.

Suddenly, I was very aware of the hole in my sock, my frizzy hair and the milk stain on my t-shirt.

'Hi,' said Conall.

He strode into the house, even though I don't think I invited him.

He took a deep breath. I folded my arms.

'I'm sorry,' he said.

'I think we've covered that.'

He stepped towards me. 'No. I'm sorry I was

a coward. With Eamonn. I'm still trying to get a handle on this whole parenting thing.'

I looked down at my orange sock, my big toe poking from the hole. Before I knew it, Conall's finger was under my chin, lifting my face up to his.

'Would you still marry a coward?' he asked.

I shook my head. 'I just want a peaceful life, Conall. I don't want more drama. And it's just *so* much.'

He smiled. 'Sofe . . . we both know we don't do easy.'

'That's hardly a winning argument,' I replied. 'What about Eamonn?'

'He'll come round.'

'So, nothing's changed,' I said.

He shook his head. 'No. But we'll change it. I think we can do that.'

And call me stupid, or naïve, but somehow, I really do believe him.

Saturday 18th December

Went to see Millie with Conall and Eamonn! Sarah said she didn't mind and that Millie likes lots of people. I was a little nervous at first because, in the car on the way, Eamonn spent most of the time complaining about one thing or another. But as soon as he saw Millie he just broke into a smile. She leapt up at him.

'Who is that?' asked Sarah, confused.

'My stepson,' I replied.

Sarah brought out snacks and she'd never looked happier or healthier. She would have her bad days, I know that. And there would be times when I'm sure maybe she, or both of us, would wonder if we'd made the right decision. But in the end, it was best to just live from one moment to the next, enjoying what was, rather than what might be.

Christmas Day

Conall's insisted that Christmas will be at his. Imagine my surprise when Mum told him the turkey wasn't as dry as it was the last time he'd made Christmas lunch. Moobs got Eamonn to play Scrabble again, even though I saw Eamonn yawn at least three times.

Seeing Millie again tomorrow. We were on

desserts (sticky toffee pudding with ice cream because not everything has to be traditional) when I said, 'So, Conall and I are looking into fostering.'

Mum let the vanilla ice cream fall from her spoon. She pursed her lips.

Eamonn smiled. 'Auntie,' he said. (He actually called my mum *Auntie*.) Even Mum seemed taken aback. 'This time we might even get two,' he added.

Took all I had not to laugh out loud.

On 1st Jan, Conall and I will get married in the mosque. Eamonn will be the unofficial best man. Sarah will come with Millie, Foz with her kids. My sister will FaceTime from Dubai.

Am very happy with the people I've chosen to spend my life with. Now, I just need to find a few more in the shape of children, and I think all will be well.

Most of the time, anyway.

Acknowledgements

Thank you to Quick Reads and The Reading Agency for the work that they do to promote adult literacy, and for asking me to be a part of such a brilliant list of writers for Quick Reads 2022. Thank you especially to Fanny Blake for allowing me to resurrect Sofia Khan and to my agent, Nelle Andrew, and editor, Eleanor Dryden, for their continued support. Many thanks also to Rosanna Hildyard for her efficient editorial management and Caroline Kirkpatrick for expert copy-editing!

Lastly, thank you to the readers, who I hope enjoy reading Sofia's story as much as I have enjoyed writing it.

About Quick Reads

"Reading is such an important building block for success"
- Jojo Moyes

Quick Reads are short books written by best-selling authors. They are perfect for regular readers and those who are still to discover the pleasure of reading.

Did you enjoy this Quick Read?
Tell us what you thought by filling in our short survey. Scan the QR code to go directly to the survey or visit
https://bit.ly/QuickReads2022

Turn over to find your next Quick Read…

A special thank you to Jojo Moyes for her generous donation and support of Quick Reads and to Here Design.

Quick Reads is part of The Reading Agency, a national charity tackling life's big challenges through the proven power of reading.

www.readingagency.org.uk
@readingagency   #QuickReads

The Reading Agency Ltd. Registered number: 3904882 (England & Wales)
Registered charity number: 1085443 (England & Wales)
Registered Office: 24 Bedford Row, London, WC1R 4EH
The Reading Agency is supported using public funding by Arts Council England.

Supported using public funding by
**ARTS COUNCIL
ENGLAND**

Find your next Quick Read:
the 2022 series

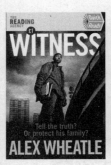

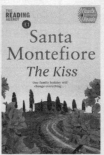

Available to buy in paperback or ebook and to borrow from your local library.

More from Quick Reads

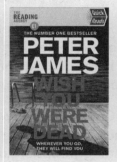

For a complete list of titles and more information on
the authors and their books visit

www.readingagency.org.uk/quickreads

Continue your reading journey

The Reading Agency is here to help keep you
and your family reading:

Challenge yourself to complete six reads
by taking part in Reading Ahead
at your local library, college or workplace
readingahead.org.uk

Join Reading Groups for Everyone to find a
reading group and discover new books
readinggroups.org.uk

Celebrate reading on World Book Night
every year on 23 April
worldbooknight.org

Read with your family as part of the
Summer Reading Challenge
at your local library
summerreadingchallenge.org.uk

For more information, please visit our website:
readingagency.org.uk